SMOKE AND THE FLAME

ACES HIGH MC - CEDAR FALLS
BOOK 2

CHRISTINE MICHELLE

Moonlit Dreams Publication

Copyright © 2019 by Christine M. Butler writing as Christine Michele
All rights reserved.

Help support authors you love by only purchasing legitimate copies of their work through trusted sources. Trusted source links and updated pricing can be found on the publisher's website at
christineandanne.com

Any similarities to persons, organizations, or places written about within these pages is purely coincidental, as this is a work of fiction.

Cover Design ©2025 Christine Michelle
ISBN: 979-8-89706-017-7

For everyone who loved Poppy and Smoke and wanted to experience the story from his point of view!

AHMC CEDAR FALLS

2

Smoke & Poppy

1. BEFORE POPPY
SIX MONTHS EARLIER

I DIDN'T KNOW WHO TO BE ANGRIER WITH AS I STARED BETWEEN MY brother and the woman I'd spent the last five years of my life with. My eyes widened in surprise as my brother finally came clean. Then I found myself turning a wicked glare on the woman in question. I couldn't even see her as the same woman I'd spent the past five years of my life with. He had to be kidding. The thought ran through my head on a loop as I tried to process the words my brother just spat out at me when I showed up on his doorstep with my long-time girl-friend in tow. Granted, I showed with her on a whim to get this confrontation out of the way once and for all.

He had liked her in the beginning and then something changed. No one would explain it to me, but every time I tried to go visit my brother, he would be too busy if I were bringing Julie along. Now I knew why, and even though it was ridiculously hard to believe that was the reason, I could see from the guilt written on her face that what he spoke was the truth.

"Let me get this straight," I finally managed to get out as I turned to Julie. "You actually asked my brother if you could upgrade to the NHL Hockey player instead of being with the firefighting biker man?"

Her lips moved, almost as if she was a fish out of water trying to draw breath. Her cheeks flamed red, and then she began to sob. "It was a long time ago, and before I fell in love with you," she admitted. I just stood there; my glare frozen on the woman who now seemed more a stranger to me than the doorman of my brother's apartment.

"You didn't think, at any point, since you made that offer to my brother that you should come clean and tell me about it?"

Her head snapped up, defiant eyes meeting mine as it did. "When do you suppose would have been a good time to do that?"

"I'm guessing the best time would have been before you made the offer to my little brother, but since you obviously weren't thinking clearly, let's go with right after you fucked up."

"You would have tossed me aside then," she admitted.

"Yeah, and according to your own admission, you didn't love me then so what would it have mattered?"

"I did like you a lot then," she tried to explain. It was a piss poor attempt as far as I was concerned.

"You liked me so much that you thought you'd wreck my relationship with my brother? Then you had the audacity to keep up a farce like you didn't understand what his problem was every single time he ditched out on anything involving you. You knew. Every single time I wondered what I had done wrong to piss my little brother off so much that he was basically alienating me, you knew you fucked that up for me. You remained silent though. You let me think I'd done something that I was incapable of fixing. All this time, it could have been fixed. I missed out on years with my brother that I will never get back, and you caused that. I raised that boy! He might as well have been my son instead of my brother, and you took that from me. From us," I indicated Kent and myself as I flipped my hand back and forth between the two of us.

The tears were falling freely down her face ruining the perfect makeup job she had done this morning. That alone made me wonder if she had changed her mind about going after my brother instead, or if she was still playing a game. She hadn't been so particular about her makeup in months, until today, when I told her we were going to surprise Kent. I narrowed my eyes on her for an instant, and then something washed over me bringing with it a sort of peace I didn't understand at the time. For the first time since I'd been with Julie, I realized I truly didn't even care if I lost her. I could not wrap my head around the sort of betrayal she had perpetrated. It was one thing to have propositioned my brother when she did, but to let me live with a fractured relationship as a result and never once speak up? That was completely unforgivable.

"Smoke," she called out as I turned my back on her.

"Don't," I told her as I picked up my bag from the floor and moved toward the door of the apartment. I turned back to glance over my shoulder. "I'm pissed at you too, man. This was avoidable. Our lives didn't have to be so fucking far apart all this time. The lost moments, the ones we can never get back, that's on you as much as it is her." My brother looked stricken by my words.

"I just wanted you to be happy, and you looked happy with her," he managed to get out.

"Yeah? How happy did I seem when you canceled our plans all those times? I wasn't fucking jumping for joy because I got to spend another weekend with my girlfriend instead of my brother who I barely got to see."

Julie sucked in a breath that we both ignored.

"I'm sorry man. You sacrificed so much for Soph and me over the years. I just wanted you to have something that was all yours."

"There is nothing in this world I want that would jeopardize the relationship I have with you or Soph. Nothing and no one. Do you understand?" Kent nodded his head and I turned to leave once more.

"Smoke?" Julie called my name again.

"You can find your own way home. We are done."

"You can't mean that. We've been together five years. This is all something that happened so long ago," she whined.

"So long ago that it still had my brother on edge and unwilling to visit with me if you were in the picture. You fucked that shit up for me. You fucked with my family. You lied. You kept your lie. You lived your lie all these years. I hope it tastes great on those lips, because you'll need that memory to get you by from here on out. Never again, Julie. What you did is un-fucking-forgivable."

With that I left. I needed time before I talked to my brother about everything because he would always be one of the most important people to me and I didn't want to say the wrong things and cause a bigger rift than he'd allowed my girlfriend to put between us. I didn't need any time between Julie and myself. All I needed where she was concerned was a whole lot of distance and space. I also needed to get back to Cedar Falls and pack my shit. I was in the market for a new place, because it wouldn't be anywhere near where she was.

2. RUN AROUND

Throwing myself into work was supposed to take my mind off cutting my girl loose and being angry with my brother. I suppose it had worked, though if I were being honest with myself it wasn't entirely necessary either. Kent and I worked our shit out. Julie and I never spoke again. That was because I meant what I said and I refused to see her, listen to her bullshit, or anything else. She had effectively been frozen out of my life and was certainly persona non grata at the club these days too. The crazy thing was, none of it bothered me. I wondered how I could have just been going through the motions with her all this time. Granted, I still hadn't formally claimed her as my old lady in all that time, even if we had been exclusive and everyone assumed it was the case. Now, I was beginning to see that maybe there was a reason for that. Julie and I had been coasting by in our relationship. With six months having gone by since I left her in my brother's apartment that day, clarity had come to me. That quick flash of relief I had experienced in my brother's place after finding out the truth had brought with it a lasting peace as well.

"Saw that new chick trying to get up on you last night at the party," Chief said as he tossed a grin my way.

"She tried," I admitted.

"Still not ready to get back on the horse?"

I shrugged my shoulders. "It's not that. Just haven't found the right horse to get on," I explained on a laugh.

"Damn, dude. When you put it like that, maybe the horses just don't want to be ridden."

"Fuck! We took the wrong track with that conversation. Now, I'm suddenly seeing flashbacks to that time you bastards dragged me to that show in Tijuana." Chief laughed his ass off then.

"Oh hell, that shit was the stuff of nightmares."

"No kidding. So, what's new with you these days. You seem to be carrying a little stress around on your shoulders."

"Just worried about Poppy," Chief explained.

"Poppy?"

"My little sister. She's still down in Georgia. I'm hearing all kinds of whispers from people down there that things aren't going so great for her. She didn't handle the anniversary of our parents' and sister's death well. There was some whole drama surrounding that, but no one will tell me what happened. Then there's Walker," he huffed out.

"Walker," I repeated the name trying to place it.

"He's a member of our Sierra High Chapter. He's also Poppy's husband, and the fucker's reportedly been stepping out on my sis."

"Damn, dude. That puts you in a tight spot with what

you can do." It did too. Having to choose between a blood sister and a club brother was going to mean he might have to break some rules if he needed to get retribution for her. I'd do it for Soph in a heartbeat if I found out her husband, Bender, was stepping out on her. Then again, just like my little brother, Kent, Soph was more than just a sibling to me. I'd helped raise her too.

"Why don't you just go get her?"

"I want her to come to me about her problems first. Right now, I'm only hearing things from a couple people."

"What the fuck? Why the wait?"

"If I force it, she'll fight me on it. If I let her come to me, she'll be living here where I can keep an eye on her – finally."

"What about in the meantime?" I asked as we hit a fuckin' pothole in the road and Chief turned a glare on me. I guess this line of questioning was distracting him from his driving.

"I have someone in place for her," he finally admitted. I wasn't sure I liked the sounds of that. Chief should have been going down to save his sister from prolonged misery rather than being on this run with me. Not to mention the fact that he mentioned having someone in place. What the hell did that mean, and how did he trust someone from down there to have his sister's back against a brother in the club? For that matter, why the hell was I ever so invested in asking all these questions? I didn't think I'd ever even met Chief's sister before, or if I had it was in passing and I didn't remember it.

We managed to find the spot where we were supposed to be meeting some of our brothers from the Tallahassee Chapter, but they hadn't arrived yet. "I'll check to see what their ETA is." I shot a text out to Court asking just that and got a response that it would be a few more minutes.

"I'll be glad when we aren't having to help Tallahassee out on these runs anymore," I finally said after we had been sitting there in silence a little too long. Unfortunately for us, this piece of shit vehicle didn't have a working radio, auxiliary port, or a fucking way to charge our phones.

"You and me both, brother. At least we get to enjoy the free pussy party when we get back," Chief commented.

I grunted out my disapproval.

"Seriously, I know we discussed the lack of decent horses earlier, but are you getting back with Julie or something?"

"Fuck no! Never look back to someone you couldn't trust the first time around, brother. Just not feeling the type of women that hang around the club and not willing to share with my brothers. Julie wasn't the one, man. I get that, but I am at a point in my life where I want to be settled. Hate to admit it, but I'm jealous of my little sister. What she and Bender have with Brantley..." I paused a moment thinking about the last time I saw my nephew. The little shit had kicked me in the shin for calling his mom stupid. I'd said it only to tease her, but he was quick to jump to her defense. "I want that. I want a family."

"Would have thought you'd be the last person who wanted that since you raised your brother and sister," he told me.

I shrugged. "I didn't mind doing it. Besides, it'll be different to have my own instead of raising siblings."

"I guess. I used to want all that too. It's what brought me to Cedar Falls in the first place."

"What changed?"

"Bitch I couldn't trust changed me. Now, I'll take no strings, and fuck the big picture. Maybe if Poppy gets shy of that dick-bag in Georgia she can finally have the kids she wants so bad and I can just spoil my little nieces and nephews."

I smiled at the thought of seeing Chief being goofy with little versions of himself running around. I'd seen him with my nephew Brant and some of the other club kids. He'd make a spectacular father one day. Shame for him to give that up because of some lying, cheating woman he scraped off before it was too late.

I tipped my head up when I heard the sputtering of a motor heading our way. "Jesus, all this business they're doing, you'd think those Florida boys could get some main-tenance done on their vehicles."

"Bite your tongue. We have to drive that shit-show all the way back home, and hope we make it." Chief laughed, but I saw there was real concern in his eyes especially when the vehicle in question sputtered and wheezed as it was put in park and turned off.

Court got out of the passenger side laughing at the looks on our faces before he slammed his open palm down on the top of the van's engine. "Aw, don't give her that look, she'll get temperamental on ya, just like a bitch."

"Fuck sake," Chief called out. "Can't you guys upgrade that shit."

Court shrugged his shoulders up and down once. "Why?

This isn't a long-haul gig. We only have a few more runs like this and we're done."

Chief shook his head back and forth. "We'll get her some maintenance done if we manage to make it all the way back to Cedar Falls without-"

"No! Do not jinx yourselves. Last time someone badmouthed Betsy here, she stopped working for a solid month," Diamond demanded as he interrupted Chief. He was one of the Florida boys, though we teased him often that he was really one of the Florida girls since he had a stripper name. He came by it as innocently as possible too. It was the fucker's last name.

"Listen sparkle-dancer," I called out to him. "We don't have time for your salvage heap to break down on us, so from now on, let's get a good clean bill of health before we do this thing, yeah?"

"Fuck you, Smoke!" Yeah, that shit always got under his skin. He hated being referred to as a stripper. Chief chuckled and then pulled his phone out of his pocket, looking down at a text that came in.

"Shit," he proclaimed and then held his finger up, asking for a minute. "You got this?"

I gave him a chin tip and watched as he walked off a little way so whoever was on the other line couldn't hear us. "What's up with that?" Court asked as he came over and slapped the keys to Betsy in the palm of my hand while I traded out the box van keys to him.

"Don't know. Might be his sister," I told him and watched as he cringed a little. "What?"

"Aw man, I was up there in Sierra High about a month

ago. Walker was running through the whores like a dying man in the desert runs through water when he finds it."

"Shit, that sounds a whole lot worse than anyone has let on to Chief," I explained.

"If I had known he wasn't aware, I would have fuckin' given him a heads up. Met Poppy a few times. She's a real sweet girl. The forever kind you don't fuck shit up with, you know?"

"Yeah, well, hopefully that's her calling her brother to come get her so she can start fresh somewhere else. He's been distracted, worried about her."

"From what I saw down there, that would be a good call. Everyone in that club knows what's going down. Not a damn one trying to talk that idiot down from his insanity except Snake, and I don't think he wants to see Walker stick it out with Poppy anyway." I kicked an eyebrow up, a question in the gesture. "Yeah, I think it's like that, but he ain't acted on nothing yet, far as I could tell."

"Well, maybe it would be best for Chief to get his ass there sooner than later. That would be a fucked situation to end up in for her."

"No shit."

Diamond interrupted any further discussion. "I'd like to enjoy soap opera hour, but we have precious cargo to get moved before the fates stop smiling on us."

"Yeah, brother. Good to see you both again. Safe ride!"

Diamond gave Betsy a little slap on her bumper. "I had a little pep talk with our girl. She might just get you back home."

"Fuckin' hell," I muttered before glancing over at Chief as

Court and Diamond drove off. They had a tail of two more Aces High members on bikes, but they hadn't gotten close enough for me to see who it was. Once they were gone, Chief hung up his cell and walked back over to me.

"Sorry about that," he offered before stuffing his cell back into his pocket. "Looks like I finally got the call. Soon as we get back, I need to head out and go get Poppy."

"Need someone with you?"

"Nah, man. You got work anyway. I'll have it handled. Apparently, she has the family house packed up and on the fuckin' market already," he told me as a giant grin bloomed across his face. "Baby sister don't play. That fucker never bothered to check on her once in the time since she kicked him out so she could have time to think. She managed to pack up the entire house. He finally shows up and sees all the boxes and lost his shit."

"She okay?"

"Aside from having her life fall apart? Yeah. Snake was there too. Nothing physical went down. He says he has a truck coming in two days. I'll be there to help load it and then I'll be driving her up. You know of a place for rent?"

"Pretty sure Hop's brother has a place just up the road from you. I'll check in on it and see if we can get her set up."

"It's empty?"

"Yeah. I just helped him remodel a bit. We yanked carpets out and refinished the wood that was underneath them. Last renters had cats that marked the carpets up. Stunk to high heaven in there."

Chief wrinkled his nose. "Maybe we need to look for something else," he mentioned.

"Nah, I promise, it's all good now. You'll see."

"Okay, if you could get that set up for me, I'd appreciate the fuck out of it."

"Not a problem, brother. You just go worry about your sister."

3. THE FLAME

I WAS ABOUT TO DRIVE ON PAST THE LITTLE COTTAGE STYLE HOUSE near the corner when I thought better of it. I knew this was the house Chief was setting his sister up in because I had arranged it for them while he went to collect her. The only vehicle in the drive now was an older, but obviously well cared for, Subaru Outback. Chief was gone since his bike was no longer there, and yet, I didn't keep going down the block. Something made me stop. I'm not that curious of a guy, but for some reason I couldn't pass by the house without meeting the sister I'd heard so much about over the past couple of weeks.

When Poppy's marriage started falling to shit, word was sent up through the chain of bickering old hens I tend to call my brothers. They were giving Chief the heads up before his sister filled him in on her troubles. I didn't really agree with him waiting on her to be forthcoming, but he knew her better than I did – which was not at all. Her man was up to no good down there in Georgia. Normally, I'd call a brother out for ratting out anyone in his MC, but in this case, it was a weird situation, and from Chief's viewpoint forgivable.

The thing that intrigued me was that Snake, the man doing the ratting in this case, was willing to go against someone who Chief claimed was the man's best friend, Poppy's husband, in order to let the brother know she needed someone to be on her side. I wasn't certain what type of woman could garner that much loyalty from a man over his brother, and ever since then, I'd paid more attention to the stories filtering in about what was going down in the Sierra High Clubhouse. I wanted to know everything. Now, I had the opportunity to see for myself what all the fuss was about, and stupidly, I was parking my bike in her driveway, about to find out. Thunder rumbled somewhere in the distance, and I knew I was pushing my luck since a storm was supposed to be rolling through in just a bit. That didn't matter. I felt compelled to be here, as strange as it sounded to admit that to myself.

I stepped up on the little front stoop and banged on the door just as a gust of wind tossed up a bit of dirt and debris from the yard. There wasn't a peephole for her to be able to see, and the window was so far over, it would no doubt leave a blind spot. That concerned me, because it was something Chief should have seen to before she moved in. I had a sister too, and I'll be damned if I'd leave her having to answer a door blind. It hadn't occurred to me what the setup was like when I was here helping to fix the place up before.

I knocked once more, thinking that whoever was in there hadn't heard me the first time, and that's when the door flew open and there stood the most beautiful woman I had ever laid eyes on. She looked almost nothing like her brother, who apparently had gotten all the Native American genes in the family while his sister looked straight off the boat from Ireland. Her auburn hair was a flaming mass on her head thanks to the streetlight's odd colored glow. Her eyes pierced mine momentarily as she tried gulping in air, but that didn't seem to be going well for her.

"You okay, honey?" I asked, taking in her heaving chest and the wild-eyed look she was throwing my way. At first, I thought she was startled by the sight of me. I knew I could be intimidating at first sight, especially if you were a single woman and I just randomly showed up on your doorstep.

"Um," she managed to get past her rapid breathing.

"I came by to see if Chief was still around," I quickly spilled out, trying to help ease her mind with the knowledge that I was friend, not foe.

"He, um," she started to say, words halted by her inability to catch her breath as she put a hand to her chest in a move that made it appear she was trying to hold herself together. I watched her a moment before sliding my phone out of my pocket, ready to call Chief and ream his ass for leaving his sister alone on her first night in a new house, new town, and new life. Surely, he knew better. From what I'd been hearing second-hand, the woman had been through enough already. The last thing she needed was to deal with this level of a freak out. Her other hand – the one not clutching her chest – shot out and waved at me though. I stopped with my phone held out in front of me, poised to text as she spoke again. "Sorry, you caught me at the start of an anxiety attack, I think."

"This happen often?" I asked while keeping a wary eye on her. Granted, I was a fireman in my day job, but I also had to know the basics of first aid and CPR. I was ready to deal with her if she went down, and if she didn't get her shit under control that might be happening sooner rather than later.

She shook her head at me instead of fainting though. "Nope, just when I move from the only home I've ever known to a new town, to look for a new job, while I'm in the middle of divorcing my cheating husband." Each of her words stabbed out into the air with painful accusation. I felt them soul deep and had to fight to keep the murderous look off of my face. I wasn't sure how Snake managed to maintain a friendship with the man who clearly destroyed this woman. I could suddenly understand why he stepped over the bounds of brotherhood where his friend was concerned in order to make sure Chief was there for his sister.

"Mind if I come in, check to make sure all is well while I'm here?" I asked her as she eyed my kutte suspiciously again. "Name's Smoke. I'm a good friend of your brother's, and he's told me a bit about your situation already, but if you need to share more with someone who isn't family, I'm all ears. Even if you don't, might help to have someone around for a bit while you adjust. Not sure what Chief was thinking leaving you alone in a strange place your first night here."

"I'm pretty sure he wasn't thinking. He was tired; so, don't hold his poor manners against him. It's been a long couple of days."

"I can imagine," I tipped my chin toward the house again, wondering if she was going to turn me away or allow me inside. I couldn't in good conscience walk away and leave her like this though. It was obvious she was having a tough time adjusting. "You gonna let me in, or I gotta call your tired brother and get his ass back over here? Whatever makes you the most comfortable, honey."

She slowly slid out of the way while checking me out as she moved. I returned the favor, taking in her clothes. She obviously chose them for comfort since she and Chief had traveled all the way up from northern Georgia today and then unloaded a truck full of shit on top of that once they got here. Still, she managed to look damn good in the everyday comfort wear while tired and mid-panic attack. It made me wonder just how much more of a knockout she would be if I had run into her fully decked out somewhere. Suddenly, I wanted to keep her hidden away here where none of my other brothers would ever see her because she was too tantalizing as is.

We spent the next couple hours getting to know one another, talking about hockey of all things. I never thought it possible to meet a beautiful southern belle who knew her shit about hockey, knew who my brother was, and still only had eyes for me. Gorgeous green eyes that shined like precious gems and drew me in closer to her. The Captain Morgan Black Label I'd had a prospect deliver was nearly gone between the two of us, and it served its purpose. All the anxiety she had earlier when I arrived was gone, and in its place was just her laughter and the glorious sight of her getting passionate about the unnecessary penalties some of my brother's teammates had taken recently.

"Oh Jeezzzzus, I'm a meth," Poppy tried to say as we

ended our latest discussion on my asshole father leaving us. She had just realized she'd been speaking with a bit of lisp for a while now. Instead, she started laughing at herself.

"She develops a speech impediment when she's drinking heavy," I spoke out loud, finding the situation funnier than I probably should. "Good to know," I told her as I watched those eyes of hers work to hypnotize and pull me in once more. Poppy spoke, almost as if reading my mind.

"Mesmerizing," she murmured, but I had to admit that I was too tuned into the puffy, rosy lips of hers to care about words anymore. I pulled her body into my mine as I wrapped an arm around her shoulder and cupped the back of Poppy's neck. I continued to pull her hips closer until she was damn near on my lap. Our lips touched, setting off an inferno everywhere they touched. It only took a brief touch before she was parting her lips for me and letting me in. I didn't hesitate. I dove right in and started to claim the woman who had me held in thrall all night. Hell, that was a lie. She had me in thrall long before I met in person. Every story I heard about her, despite her recent shitty circumstances, was one that painted a picture of the woman I'd been dreaming of calling my own all my life. Her silky tongue met and tangled with my own, and her sweet, beautiful moan had my hard as fuck cock twitching in my pants and begging for release. I knew in that moment I would do whatever it took to make her mine.

Our mouths were still locked in a heated kiss as I took the liberty of learning her body, the feel of her curves, and the smoothness of her skin. I ran my fingertips up and down her ribs, moving closer and closer to her breasts that were overflowing the bra she had on. It was one that was made for comfort, cotton instead of satin or lace like most women wore to impress. That wasn't Poppy though. Not that my arrival hadn't been a complete surprise for her anyway, but I had a feeling she was the type of woman who wore comfortable well, and made it seem hotter than any expensive lingerie could possibly look. The bra was unclasped, and I was dragging it down her arms before I could even put anymore thought into how sexy she might look in it. The garment no sooner hit the floor than her hands were on me, tugging at my shirt to get it off me and join her clothing that already littered the floor of the living room.

"Please, tell me you have a bed set up?" I questioned as each word caused my lips to graze gently back over her own. She pointed and I took off to the little hallway that housed three doors. The one in the center was the bathroom which left two choices.

"Left or right, babe?"

"Left," she hissed as I lifted her, and she wrapped her legs around my waist allowing me to carry her into the bedroom. Thank fuck, there was a bed. Not that the lack of one would have stopped me, but it would make what we were about to do a whole lot more comfortable.

I managed to put her down gently onto the bed while I tugged my jeans down and used my feet to pull the denim material free from my legs. I left them puddled there on the floor as she took in the view of my body standing over her. I kneeled on the edge of the bed and leaned in placing a quick kiss on her thigh, nipping gently with teeth as I moved further up. My hands were sliding slowly along her outer thighs until I managed to get her to spread her legs wider to accommodate my body between them. Once she was relaxed and open, I moved my hands in place on either side of her hips and slid the last bit of clothing keeping her from view. The white cotton panties she'd had on slid down her legs and I tugged to remove them from her feet before tossing them aside and quickly moving back into a position where I could take all of her in before I dove in with my shoulders sliding between her thighs, and breathed warm air all over her slick flesh. Then I flattened my tongue and took a delicious swipe of her most intimate part before I made it up to the little bundle of nerves at the top that was begging to be sucked on. That was exactly what I did. I sucked it into my mouth and nipped gently with teeth causing her to whimper.

"Shit!" She managed to articulate before throwing her head back as her eyes fell closed and she dragged her fingers through my hair. She was holding me to her, and I didn't mind one bit, because I'd just figured out what heaven tasted like. It was Poppy's sweet musk with a hint of salt, and those sweet as fuck whimpering noises that kept making my cock stand further at attention. I wanted to make this damn good for her, because I had a feeling it was the first time she'd been able to let go and just feel in a long time. The truth of the matter was, I didn't know how long I could hold out so I trailed my hands up her sides until I had her tits cupped firmly in my grasp as I went to town fucking and sucking her pussy with my tongue. I rasped my bearded face across her sensitive clit every time I dipped down to pump my tongue inside of her and scoop out all of her juices. As she grew closer to her own climax, she also became rougher with her demands, tugging and pulling at my hair to make sure I focused my attention exactly where she needed me.

Seconds that felt like hours ticked by as I refused to let up until I felt her thighs begin to shake at my shoulders and then I sucked deeply on her clit as I pinched down hard on both of her nipples sending her tumbling over into a climax I could feel shake her to her core.

"Shit, holy," she huffed out. "Jesus, God." I snickered against her as she had her religious experience and finally eased up on the hold she had on my hair. I wouldn't have been surprised to find that she took a few strands away with her. Just as she release me I heard my name roll off of her tongue like a prayer. "Ungh, Smoke!"

"Honey," I called out in response as I worked my way back up her body, planting open-mouthed kisses as I went. Easing inside of her was something else. She was so hot, slick, and fucking tighter than I'd felt a woman in a long as fuck time. It had to be everything in combination, because this was something new for me. "Never before," I managed to tell her before I increased the tempo of my thrusts, trying to feel every part of her that I could. Hell, I was trying to get as deep into her as was humanly possible, because this connection I was feeling was something else. At the risk of sounding like a bitch – it was fucking magical.

"Smoke, I'm-"

"I know, honey. Feel it. Let go, because it's not going to be the last one tonight. Not done with you yet." I meant every word as I felt her do exactly as I commanded. I pounded into her as her pussy contracted around me and then when she thought she was done; I flipped her ass over and took her from behind as she purred for me on all fours. I pounded into her roughly, taking what I wanted. As I hunched over her back and held her tightly around her waist, I pulled on one of her nipples and then reached down and began paying attention to her clit as well while I hammered into her relentlessly. Finally, I managed to send her over the edge once more before I finally found my own release.

"Honey," I whispered into Poppy's ear as I collapsed against her backside riding that last bit of momentum to the end. "Let go, sweetheart. Can't. Hold. Onnnn," I growled to her as I felt her clamp down around my cock just before I let loose and found my own release deep inside of her.

"Fuck, honey, never in my life," I tried to say before I realized that I was probably squishing her the way I was draped all over her back as we came crashing down to the bed. "Sorry," I laughed.

"Not a damn thing to be sorry for. I'm amazed you held it together as long as you did."

"Shh," I hummed in her ear as I pulled her close and covered our rapidly cooling with her blanket. Her hair was sweat-slicked across her face and I gently brushed it away, exposing her beautifully flushed face to me. "Get some sleep, honey," I demanded in the softest of tones while trying to lure her into a restful sleep. Judging from everything I knew about her situation and the panic attack I'd walked in on her having at the start of our night, I'd say she desperately needed it.

"Mmm," was her only response before I felt her body go slack in my arms. There was one thing I knew for sure, and that was that Poppy was made for me. There was no chance in hell I'd be letting her get away. I didn't care if everyone in our lives thought it was too soon. Hell, I'd be lying if I didn't acknowledge the small part of myself who thought I was crazy thinking this shit, but I couldn't help it. Every minute I'd spent in her presence had been perfect so far.

4. STEPPING IN IT

Babysitting duty was going to kill my spirit today. I loved my nephew more than the world, but I'd forgotten I was supposed to sit with him while his parents went and had some alone time without him. I had no clue that I was going to not only meet Poppy last night, but that she would end up being the whole fucking package. She was exquisite in every way, from her gorgeous, yet unassuming appearance to her intelligence and creativity. Then there was the fact that she could talk hockey with me and get truly excited about the player's stats and not just their height, weight, and sexy scruff factor as Poppy put it when she was joking about the only way she had been able to get girls in her past to discuss the sport with her.

I glanced back one more time as I hopped in Bender's Ford Expedition and when I turned back, it was to see the bastard brother-in-law of mine grinning his head off.

"Finally met Chief's sister, did ya?"

"You could say that," I managed to get out without giving anything away.

"She's a looker. Chief's going to have his hands full trying to keep the men off of her."

"The fuck he is!" I yelled at him.

The bastard chuckled. "Yeah, that's what I thought. She already has you under her spell, brother."

"Whatever," I grumbled.

The smile was swept away to be replaced with concern. "Just be careful. Her split has been ugly, but it's still new and I'm pretty sure they've clocked the better part of a decade together."

"I am aware of all those things."

"I just don't want to see you get hurt if he comes around begging for her back and she goes. You know how it can be with the women who have been around the club a while. They think they're mad about the cheating, but then they decide they can get over it, because they'll miss the life too much. Or the man."

"Trust me when I say I don't think she would be one of those. If it turns out that way, you can say you warned me when I'm crying in my cornflakes and can't get out of bed, okay?" Sure, it was sarcasm, but honestly, if all of my days with Poppy ended up even a fraction of how well our night had turned out, that didn't seem a far-fetched result if she decided to hightail it back to Sierra High, Georgia.

Before long, I found myself confiding in Bender about my night with Poppy. He pulled into a convenience store parking lot and pulled into a back into a parking space before putting the Expedition in park and turning to me. "So, what exactly did you say to her about why you were leaving again? You said you promised Soph you'd watch the kid?" His questions bothered me for some reason that I couldn't put my finger on.

"That's what I fuckin' said," I told him, feeling my temper rise a bit.

He laughed. "Shit, you're gonna have some 'splainin' to do, my brother."

"What? Why?"

"She probably had all kinds of ideas about who that kid was to you and who Soph was," Bender told me and suddenly it hit me. The panic set in and I was about to get him to turn around so I could rectify that situation, but then I remembered Chief was there too.

"Her brother will set her straight," I informed him.

"You sure about that? If I were Chief and I walked in on the two of you all post-coital this morning, I would probably fuck with you hardcore through her."

"If it wasn't Poppy, and she hadn't been through everything she's recently gone through, I'm sure you would be right. There's no way he's going to leave her in doubt of what happened last night just to fuck with me though. That would be cruel to her."

"I see your point. I guess you got lucky this time. Word to the wise, if you're ever talking about a kid and another woman to someone you only just started dating, fucking, or whatever you two are doing; there probably needs to be some sort of explanation as to who those people you mentioned are before you up and run out of breakfast."

I ran my hand nervously through my hair, because

honestly, I should have known better. Before I could get lost in my own thoughts of Poppy and where I thought we were going to be headed with our little new-found friendship, my brother-in-law got a call.

"What's up babe?" I knew immediately it was my sister. "Seriously, still no?" Bender sighed, disappointed in something she was saying. "Okay, I'll let him know. No, it's okay. Another time. I'll be back as soon as I drop Smoke off."

"Drop me off?"

"Yeah, sorry, man. Your sister wasn't exactly feeling well this morning, but she swore it was okay to pick you up because she thought it would pass." He lifted a shoulder in agitation.

"I'm guessing it hasn't passed?"

"Not sounding like it, so I'm just going to drop you at your bike. Maybe you can catch back up with Poppy and Chief?"

"Yeah, okay."

I was on my bike at a stop light when I felt the vibrations. I pulled it out at the next stop to take the call. "Yo! What's up, Shep?"

"Smoke," he called me by my road name instead of my actual name which immediately put me on edge. "I have a problem. Not sure if you can help, but I'd sure as fuck appreciate it if you could."

"What's going on?"

Shep gave a quick rundown of how his mom's latest asshole had put her and his sister in danger, and they needed help getting out.

"I'm on my way to your place. Give Bender a call and let

him know. His plans got canned today, and I'm sure he'd be down for helping too."

"Thanks." I hung up and took off, heading in his direction again. I was half way there when I felt my phone vibrating. I cursed myself for not having the damn thing paired up to the Bluetooth in my helmet yet. I had just bought the new phone a couple days ago and still hadn't bothered to do it. Then again, I didn't usually get this many calls that I wanted to answer. When I had been with Julie, I tended to ignore my phone until I got somewhere because I didn't want her nagging about when I would finally make it home.

At the next light, I yanked the phone back out of my pocket, and thank fuck I did, because the asshole coming up behind me wasn't slowing the fuck down. I caught sight of him in my mirror and just barely managed to move out of the way before he would have taken me out. Still ended up dropping my phone and having the bastard run it over. "Mother fucker!" I growled wishing I had the time to chase the son of a bitch down. I took note of the traffic cam, and the fact that I'd be putting in a call to the boys in blue to find that son of a bitch for me. He deserved far more than the ticket the camera was going to throw him. Waiting to get his ass kicked until I had time to do it would just make it that much sweeter.

It didn't take long to get to Shep's place after that, mostly because the shot of adrenaline from almost being taken out by a careless asshole driving a cage was still riding my body. Being charged up meant I wasn't a laid back rider.

"That was quick, what the hell happened? You answered my call and then everything went dead."

"Fucking moron took out my phone on the road, almost

took me out had I not seen him in time. Thanks for the call, you literally probably just saved my fuckin' life."

"No shit?" Shep asked, eyes wide, as he took in my appearance. "Yeah, you're jacked up right now. Come on, you can grab a drink, and we'll go over what you think I need to do to help them out before I hit the road."

"Before we hit the road," I tell him. "I'm not leaving you to handle this shit on your own. Your girls need moved, we'll get them gone from that situation and make sure the fucker knows they aren't to be trifled with again."

He glanced down at his phone and grimaced. "Might need to get on the road and head that way sooner than later. I'm not sure how much longer they have before someone gets hurt."

"Give me your phone a minute," I tell him and he hands it over without a complaint. I quickly shoot messages to Bender, Chief, and Ghost telling them what's going on. Ghost says he doesn't mind sanctioning the club assist, and Chief shoots back a message that Wren will be joining too.

I turned to Shep. "All right, Bender, Chief, and Wren are meeting us here and then we'll ride out. You taking your truck in case you need something to put the women in to get them back here?"

"I guess I better. That way I can grab some of their shit too, hopefully. Depends on the situation we end up rolling into."

"Don't worry about that. We'll get as much of their shit as we can fit in the truck. We'll pack the fuckin' cab if need be and your mom and sister can hop on the back of one of the bikes."

Shep laughed at that. "I'd like to see any of you attempt to convince my mom, of all people, to just hop on the back of your bike for the ride home." He shook his head and chuckled as we moved to the garage and he rolled the truck out, securing his bike inside. By the time he was finished and had everything locked up, the rest of my brothers had arrived, and we all headed out to what we thought would be a simple run to help a friend. If only we had known how wrong we were.

We rolled up to the place where Shep's mom had moved to after hooking up with her latest loser. I could already feel that shift in the air that signaled things were not going to be as simple as we thought when we rolled out. Suddenly, I was thankful so many of my brothers had come along for the ride. It wasn't even that it looked like there were too many people here to handle. My gut was sending that tingling warning through my body, telling me shit was not as it seemed.

"Something isn't right," I finally stated out loud as I took my helmet off.

"I feel it too," Bender put in.

"Same," Wren called out as he killed his engine.

Shep looked back and forth between us and it was clear he didn't get the same gut reaction. I wasn't sure if that was just because he'd never been in some of the situations we'd faced as a club, or if it was because he was too close to the situation since his mom and sister had reached out for help.

"Did they say if they were alone?"

Shep tipped his head to the side, indicating a busted old truck sitting there. "Looks like the asshole is home."

I had that itch to text Poppy and make sure she was okay, or let her know that I was. She wasn't even my old lady yet, and besides, my phone was toast. I'd dropped it and crushed it on my way to Shep's. I turned to ask Chief if he could text her, but the front door to the house flew open and a wide-eyed, crazy looking fucker stood there with a shot gun aimed in our direction.

"Don't know who the fuck all of you are, but you need to get gone from here!"

A female voice screamed out, "Shep!" It sounded muffled and distant, and we all realized what that meant almost immediately. "I've got the back door," Wren called out as he and Chief took off in that direction.

"Where the fuck do you think you're going?" The crazy fucker with the shotgun yelled at them as he brought the muzzle around, tracking their movements. Wren and Chief ignored the threats and I moved in. I shouldered his arm with the shotgun upward, so that if he pulled that trigger the shot would fly to the sky before letting gravity take its course, putting our guys in the clear. Then I had to get clear quickly, because Shep had come up and kicked the man's knee out from under, dropping him immediately.

"What the fuck are you doing with my mom and sister?" Shep seethed at the man.

Bender was by my side, collecting the fallen weapon, and helping to drag the bastard inside. We did not need an audience, or worse, someone with a cell phone standing in their window witnessing what looked like us breaking into a home and assaulting the residents. I turned to check to see if there was anyone we would need to talk to once we were done here, but all I noticed was a black suburban with windows tinted so heavily, they were beyond well illegal in this state. "Bender," I called out and tipped my head. He saw it and gave me the nod indicating he understood too. If nothing else, we had witnesses to what we'd just done. The fact that the witnesses looked shady as fuck though, did not bode well. There was more going on here than Shep thought.

Once we were inside, Wren and Chief met us in the living room with two terrified women and another man. The women were a mirror of one another with exception of the fact that one was obviously about 20 or so years older than the other. Shep's mom had aged well, and his sister was a dead ringer for the woman.

The man, on the other hand, did not look as though he belonged at all. Every inch of skin that wasn't covered by clothing was dripping with ink. His face, while not completely covered, also had tattoos present. I couldn't make out most of it, as they looked to be symbols and shit written in another language. If I had to guess, I'd say Slavic, based on the man himself and the way it looked. That didn't mean I could translate the least bit of it.

"Who the fuck are you?" Shep asked the man who only smirked at him response. Then he turned to the idiot that Bender and I still had a hold of. "Who the fuck is that? And what the hell is going on here, you piece of shit?"

The asshole we had hold of spit at Shep's boots. He missed in the pathetic attempt to disrespect the man so I slapped him around for being stupid. Nothing pissed a grown ass man off more than being bitch slapped by another man. He growled out in frustration, so I slapped him again.

"Answer Shep's questions asshole, or we'll get creative with how we get the truth out of you."

We all watched as the fucker glanced in the direction of the other man and clammed up at seeing the ruthless look on his face. He promised to do more harm to the man with one look than we could ever threaten. It didn't matter that he'd been captured too. You wouldn't know it by the menacing air he was putting off.

"He sold us to that guy," Lindsay, Shep's sister, cried as she pointed to the tatted up bastard that was now staring daggers at her.

"Get that fucker out of here," I told Wren. He nodded his head and hit the guy with the butt of his gun. The man dropped like a sack of potatoes and, once he was out, they managed to find shit to tie him up with in the kitchen. Wren stuck around in the kitchen to stand guard and keep an eye on the back door while the rest of us gathered in the living room to figure out exactly what the fuck was going on.

"Now, why would a man sell his wife and stepdaughter to some inked-up thug?" I asked. Chad Montgomery, the man in question, looked up at me and started laughing.

"You think I'm afraid of you boys and your little bikes you ride? I'm not."

"He owes money," Tammy pipped up.

"Shut your fucking mouth, you stupid cunt!"

"You can kiss my ass, Chad! You just sold my daughter to pay off your gambling debts!" Tammy shrieked across the living room at her piece of shit husband.

"Sold you too, bitch!"

"Yeah?" she asked, smugly. "How'd that work out for ya?"

That was when the dick blanched, and finally realized the situation he was in. Either way, he wouldn't be coming out of this shitstorm alive. If we didn't take him out – and we would – the assholes he was dealing with sure as fuck would be back to try to claim what they thought was their rightful payment for his debts.

After I let it sink for a minute, I gripped his greasy blond hair and pulled his head back so he could look me in the eyes. "Now that you figured out your lot in life – what's left of it – maybe you want to start talking? We'll make it quick and relatively painless if you do. Those other fucks don't look like they'll make it painless or quick for you."

"I can't. They'll know I talked."

"So, you'll be dead," Bender laughed. "What are they going to do? Bring you back?"

"They'll go after my wife and kids," he shouted as the acrid smell of urine started to fill the room.

"Did you just piss yourself?" I asked as my nose wrinkled up at the smell.

"You already sold your wife and kid to them!" Shep yelled.

"That cunt don't mean shit to me, and that little bitch ain't no kid of mine," Chad snarled.

"What?" Tammy shrieked.

"That's right, cunt. We ain't legally married. I already have a real woman back home. We were just taking a break when I met you. Figured I could have you on the side, but fuck if you weren't too much work. Thought you'd help pay some of the debt off since you work at the hospital, but I didn't realize you were fucking downing in those credit cards."

"You sorry ass motherfucker!" She screeched and before anyone knew what was happened she jumped up, grabbed the shotgun we'd tossed to the side, and shot the fucker right in the head.

"Jesus!" I yelled as I jumped back out of the way. Bender swore and dove out of the way too. Shep managed to tackle his mother, a little too late.

"Momma?" Lindsay called out, shocked and sounding far younger than she looked at first glance only moments ago.

"Oh God! What did I do?" Tammy started to wail.

"Eto nereal'no," We heard the other man mutter amidst his own laughter.

"You have a basement here?" Wren asked from the kitchen?"

"Yes," Tammy said as she shook like a leaf. Obviously, shock had begun to set in either over her circumstances or the fact that she'd just shot and killed her fake husband. I didn't know if that was the case, but it was my best guess.

"Let's get this mess down there, too," I told Bender. He nodded his head and helped me move the body as Chief did his best to shield Lindsay's view of what was happening. Not that it mattered all that much after she was nearly abducted and watched her mom shoot the man she thought was her stepfather.

"Do we have to find his family now?" Tammy was asking.

"You will do no such thing. That's for the police to do, if they can identify him. I'm thinking the woman already knows he's a peace of shit, considering they were on a long enough break that he was able to set up house with a new woman and be involved enough with you that you were willing to marry him."

I didn't see or hear Tammy's response, but I knew Chief was about to put the fear of God and the Aces High MC into both women. If they talked, and our involvement became known, that would be a problem for our club that was damn near ready for all its chapters to go 100 percent legit. We had done our time as one percenters and that time was coming to an end, because there was just too much loss involved. The risks didn't outweigh the reward in this day and age.

Once we had the body moved to the basement, we called up for Wren to send the other asshole down. He did, with a swift kick to the ass, the dipshit tumbled down the steps and landed in a heap at our feet. I knelt beside the man and realized, by the odd angle of his neck, that we weren't going to get to question him either.

"What the fuck, Wren?"

"Sorry man, he was getting feisty."

"Well, he's dead now," I informed him as he came down the steps to see for himself.

"Shit, I didn't mean for that to happen."

"Let's get some pictures of his tats. Maybe they'll lead us to whoever he was working for. My best guess though is Russians. That's what this shit looks like," I told them pointing out a few of the tattoos. "We had that one guy before," I started to say, but couldn't think of his name.

"Yeah, I remember. He wanted to be a prospect, right?"

"He was a hang around for a while until he ended up dead," I confirmed. "He had similar shit inked on him."

"Okay, well it gives us a jumping off point," Bender mentioned as he started pouring what looked like lighter fluid on the two bodies. "Go on upstairs and give me a shout when everyone's clear. I'll have this place torched in no time."

Thankfully, the house was not sitting terribly close to any of the others in the neighborhood. "Let's go get the girls back home and hidden away for a while."

Once we were far enough away from the house, we let Bender know it was okay to light it up, and he took off too, catching up to us quickly, before we managed to haul ass out of there. We had managed to get some of the girls' things into the truck before we took off, so at least they wouldn't have to start over completely. We were clear of the area before we found a storage unit to put their belongings in, and then we doubled back and headed in the opposite direction of Cedar Falls. The stop to unload their shit was necessary because we didn't want to be hauling a bunch of shit if we ended up with a tail of any kind. We managed to roll through Ohio and Pennsylvania, stopping there overnight at a piece of property we had with a few barns on it. We had converted one of them into a pretty sick shelter that was housed underground, beneath one of the barns. They all just looked like aging, decrepit buildings. As soon as we were all rested, we headed out again, stopping each day, for three days, in a new place. It was all done to throw the trail.

From our last stop, we separated and went in different directions with the same destination in mind. I Was pretty sure Wren was headed back to report in with Ghost about the possible blowback from our trip. Bender and Chief took off on their own on the last day too. I helped Shep get the girls settled into a hotel just outside of Cedar Falls until he could figure out what to do with them. I wasn't entirely sure four hours away from the scene of the crime was enough. Luckily, he agreed with me.

Once everyone was settled, the only thing on my mind was getting back to Poppy. Little did I know, I was going to have some explaining and groveling to do since I hadn't had a phone with me, and apparently Chief hadn't contacted her either. I knew a way to make it all up to her though. A couple days after we got back, I took her to her first Penguins game in Pittsburgh. Unfortunately, we weren't really able to do more than say hello to my brother afterward, but that didn't seem to matter to Poppy. What mattered was us being there together, and it only endeared me to her even more.

5. FINICKY FAMILY

THE HOCKEY GAME HAD GONE A LONG WAY TOWARD WINNING Poppy's good graces back. None of us had heard anything down the wire about what happened with Shep's family either, which was a fucking miracle, and left us all feeling a bit on edge at the same time. There was no way, if this had been mafia related as we had originally assumed, that they would leave it. We all knew that war was a possibility on our horizon, and still, we were all determined to go about living our lives as if there was nothing any different brewing some-where in the background. Sure, we were all a little more vigi-lant, but it wasn't stopping us from living. I was in the process of living and working my latest shift at CFFRD when I glanced down at my new cell phone and saw a message there from my sister, Soph.

> Soph: What are you bringing tomorrow?

> Smoke: ?

I had no clue what she was on about now. I was probably supposed to babysit Brantley again and forgot or something.

Sophie: Please, tell me you're not coming with the tramp from Georgia!

Smoke: Whoa! What the fuck, Soph?

Sophie: After Julie, that's really what you want to hook yourself to? An already married woman?

Smoke: Soph? What the hell is going on, and where do you expect I'll be tomorrow?

Sophie: Club cook out tomorrow, idiot.

Smoke: Shit, I forgot all about that.

Sophie: No shit, Sherlock!

Smoke: I guess I'll be stopping by.

Sophie: Without a guest, right?

Smoke: This is the only warning you will get, little sister. Check your attitude! My decisions are just that. Mine!

Sophie: Fine, but don't say I didn't warn you when it all blows up in your face and she runs back to Georgia with her ex. That's how club bitches roll, and you know it. They find out he's cheating, they leave. Then they miss club life, and go right back. All forgiven.

> Smoke: You seriously have no clue what you're talking about, so stop.

I couldn't believe my sister had the nerve to talk about Poppy like that. Normally, Soph didn't have a mean bone in her body so I didn't know what the hell was wrong with her. Just to be sure I wouldn't have any trouble out of her, I sent a text to her man, my club brother.

> Smoke: You need to put your woman on a short leash tomorrow. The shit she just had to say about Poppy – Chief's sister – was completely vile.

> Bender: Shit. I'll have a talk with her.

> Smoke: Good luck with that. She gets in Poppy's face tomorrow though, there will be problems. The woman is club even if she isn't with me or her ex. She's club because Chief would never allow her to be tossed aside.

> Bender: I know it. I'll make sure your sister behaves.

I shook my head as I glanced down at his message. I didn't know when exactly my world had flipped upside down, but having to sic my sister's old man on her was something completely new. I didn't get much time to contemplate that though because we were up, and I had to get to my engine and roll out.

"Two alarm," someone called out as I rushed into my gear. Shit, that meant we were probably looking at a long call. Two alarms were rare in our area since everything was so spread out, but when we got them, they went one of two ways. Either the extra units were barely necessary, or we were quickly upgraded to a three alarm because of proximity to other buildings or the size of the original fire. It was obvious by the time we rolled up to the scene that this fire would fall into the latter category. I pulled in a deep breath and prepared myself for a long night just before I jumped into the action.

WHEN I finally got to knock off of my shift, I was already fifty-two minutes into my day off. We got slammed back to back with the two-alarm fire that became a three alarm before we even started, then there was a traffic accident followed by an overturned chemical truck we had to be on standby for. We had just rolled in from yet another accident where we had to use the jaws to get the driver out. I was beat, my muscles ached, and honestly all I wanted to do was ride out to Poppy's place and wrap myself around her for a little while.

Then I remembered I needed to check in with Gray since I was finally done with the damn shift from hell. He had texted me about needing to celebrate while I was in Pittsburgh with Poppy. I figured I better do it before I left work because once I got my woman back in my arms, I wasn't about to let her go. I had the next two days off and nothing on the horizon with club business that would need to be handled. That meant I was going to be all hers for two whole days. I just hoped she was ready for that since we were still blurring the 'just friends' and 'friends with benefits' line a bit.

If she wasn't still married and dealing with all the shit her ex-asshole had put her through, I would have already claimed her properly. The fact of the matter was that going at her pace didn't seem to be the easy task it should have been. I wanted more, and I was selfish enough to want it all right the fuck now. I shook the thought off, knowing it couldn't happen that way, and I texted Gray.

> Smoke: What's up with the need to celebrate? Just got off shift and want to spend the next two days off with Poppy, but if you need me, I'll see if we can block out some time for you.

It took about twenty minutes for Gray to respond.

> Gray: Fuck! Those bathrooms are nasty down the back hall, dude.

I couldn't help the laugh that forced its way out of my exhausted body. I remembered the days when I was a prospect. At least I had been much younger back then. Gray was a full-grown man and having to clean up after clubhouse rancidness was not something full grown men easily stooped to. That's why those shit details showed a man's mettle.

> Smoke: Remember those days – not fondly. What's going on?

Gray: Asked Ghost – the club – to help me with a poker run to raise some cash for Beth and Abby. Ghost said absul-fuckin-lutely. It's on, already been planning.

Smoke: Outstanding. Let me know what we can do to help.

Gray: Can Poppy bake or cook? I want to get a bake sale type thing going at some of the stops along the run to help with raising more funds. Thinking about having the old ladies set up a swap meet style booth or table too towards the end. Then an auction.

Smoke: Damn, man, you're going all in. Sure, you don't see more in Beth than just a man trying to help?

Gray: Nah. She's a sweet lady, her daughter is a cutie, but I think of her more as a sister that needs help since half her family just died.

Smoke: Headed to Poppy now. I'll give her your number. Sure, she'd be glad to help out.

Gray: Thanks, dude.

I chuckled at the last text. He just couldn't help himself. Poor asshole was going to get landed with the Surfer moniker whether he liked it or not, and it was his own damn fault.

That was all the thought I was willing to give Gray though. It was amazing what he was doing for a woman and her child that he only met because he was part of the emergency crew that showed up after the accident she was involved in. I had been there too, but in a different capacity. I'm not sure I wouldn't have reacted the same way if I had been in his shoes, and in such close proximity to the woman's heartache. She had lost her husband and two older children in that wreck. Both fire and rescue were trained that we were not supposed to get involved with the victims once we were relieved from our duties. Sometimes, that just wasn't possible.

In Gray's case, he had been there with his hands on the woman, trying to stabilize her when she'd become conscious again. The first thing she saw was one of the dead children, then her husband, and she had lost her shit. Gray had talked her down and he stuck with her and the baby that survived through the whole ordeal. Then, he went a step beyond and started going to check in on her and the baby, knowing they didn't have anyone, and that it was impossible with Beth's injuries for her to take care of certain things.

Gray was one of the good ones. Even so, I chucked him to the back of my mind, because the only thing I wanted more than the air that kept me alive was to be in Poppy's arms. I wish I could play it cool and pretend I didn't have intense feelings toward her from the very start, but I did. It was also unlike anything I'd ever experienced before and that was a revelation in and of itself considering how long I attached myself to my ex. How had I allowed myself to be lulled into the tedium of relationship that could be described that way? Hell, how had my family ever thought I was happy in that existence? More importantly, how the hell was I going to get

Poppy to go along with the game plan of her and I being together for the long haul?

Doubt niggled at my mind making me wonder if she'd even let me crawl into bed and curl up with her once I got to her house. I had just been heading there because of this desire I had to wrap my body around hers and take comfort from the warmth she gave so freely without even realizing she was doing it. It never dawned on me until I was pulling in her driveway that she might not feel the same.

I'd just have to convince her to allow me to stay there. Her ex had done a number on her, and I was afraid that us meeting so soon after would have repercussions I wasn't going to be happy with. The texts my sister had sent me earlier came to mind. While I was angry with Soph for the way she chose to deliver her message, it wasn't honestly anything I hadn't already considered.

What if Poppy ended up back in Georgia?

What if her ex won her over somehow?

I wasn't sure how I would handle that, because I was already well and truly attached to the woman. Even though I had my own concerns I thought Soph was wrong. What did I know, though? My last woman had come on to my brother, offering to 'trade up' to him because she thought he was the better choice, and because he never told me about it I stayed with her for four more years. I shook my head. I didn't see Poppy being that type of person. It turned out that all my doubts were for nothing. She had no problem with me coming in and getting comfortable with her for a while. I'd take what I could get. For now.

6. INTENTIONS

PUTTING POPPY ON THE BACK OF MY BIKE AGAIN THE NEXT DAY FELT all kinds of right. I never had an easy ride with Julie in the beginning because she wouldn't listen to me about how to lean with me through curves or to hang on and not bounce around when she saw something that excited her. Maybe, it wasn't fair to compare the two because Poppy had years of riding bitch with another man. I didn't like to think about it, but it was true. Before that, she also had a biker brother, and from what Chief told me, their father had always had a bike when they were growing up too, even though he'd never been part of a club. Poppy was born and raised for this life in her own way. Julie never had been. It was only in the few months before we split that my rides with Julie on the back were smooth and unlike the headache they had been in the beginning.

Part of that might have been that she had come to terms with being an old lady, even though I'd never made that official. She'd just decided that it wasn't such a bad life and I wasn't so much the runner-up anymore. Not for the first time, I wondered what I had been thinking sticking it out so long with a woman I wouldn't even consider calling my old lady. Now that I found someone, I wanted to do that with, it wasn't possible. Even thought he'd been a dick, cheated on her, and whatever else, Poppy's ex was still a club brother and still legally married to the woman I wanted. I could think about claiming her for myself, but that's all it could ever be until things were settled between them. Even then, I wasn't sure how the club would react if Walker put up an argument that she was to be off limits to club brothers.

Truth be told, if this were any other situation, I would stand to lose my kutte for going after Poppy when things weren't settled with her previous old man. Actually, even if they were. I'd only ever heard of a club brother picking up what another had scraped off and still remaining in the club one other time. That was with our man Hopper when he got rid of his son's mom because she was too much to handle. They hadn't ever been married though. Iceman, the Dakotas Chapter President, had picked her up and married the woman. He didn't having Hopper's son around as his step son, but if rumors were true, the man regretted his decision to get involved with Hopper's ex immensely.

With Poppy's situation, it helped that Chief was also in the club and he made it known to our chapter that he'd put his sister's happiness up against our brother from another chapter who fucked around on her. If I was the reason for her happiness he wasn't going to complain.

No sooner did we get there and Poppy was hopping off

my bike, than Heavy was calling out to me. "Thought you didn't let bitches ride on your bike anymore, man?" The asshole was about to eat his own words, and maybe a few teeth talking about her like that though.

"Call her a bitch again and we'll be talkin' out back in the shed," I answered back. He nodded, and I could see from the inquiring look on his face that he wanted to know what was up with that, but I was just ticked enough with him to not want to answer. It didn't matter that it was Chief's sister, or the woman I planned to claim as soon as it was possible, he had no right to start a woman's day out making her feel like shit. Calling a woman, that a brother brought by, a 'bitch' while comparing her to others was not an easy start to a day that you want to go smooth. Still, I tipped my head to Poppy and we both moved toward where Heavy was standing with Hold 'Em and Crutch.

"This is Poppy," I introduced.

"Poppy?" Crutch asked before turning his full attention to the woman in question. "You're Chief's sister, right?"

"That I am," she answered him with one of her beautiful smiles.

"Oh!" Heavy chimed in. "Chief asked you to bring her by? I'm assuming that means he's bringing one of his bitches then?" Fucking Christ, someone needed to put their foot up Heavy's ass. Pretty sure I growled out my response, but I couldn't honestly tell you, because I was that pissed off with the man.

"Poppy's with me because she's mine!" I glared at each man standing there, even though it had only been Heavy who pissed me off. "Don't know what Chief's up to or if he's bringing anyone," I clarified just before I noticed Hold 'Em grinning big at my woman.

"Oh, hey!" Poppy called out excitedly.

"Hey Poppy," he answered back. "How's that monster of yours?"

Her sweet as fuck laugh made all my anger drain away as I just took her in while she talked to my future brother. There was no doubt our prospect would be moved up in the ranks to full member, and soon.

"He's good, although he didn't seem too happy to be left behind today," she told him.

It hit me then that Hold 'Em was a prospect and Poppy was new to town, not having been to visit Cedar Falls in quite a while before she came to live here. "You know Hold 'Em?" The minute the words were out of my mouth I remembered the fact that Hold 'Em had been the one to check on her when Chief and I were busy helping Shep.

"Yeah, Chief brought him by when he got back from the run the other day and realized he'd left me without a way to communicate with anyone."

"Take it you met Bubba?" I asked him, which caused the man to sputter out a nervous sounding laugh. "Damn near pissed my pants meeting Bubba, thought he was gonna fuckin' tear my leg off," he admitted. I turned to Poppy for an explanation.

She shrugged her shoulders. "There was a strange man on my front porch, and it made me nervous. I'm sure Bubba felt that and was feeding off my energy."

"Like that Bubba was doing his job, honey," I told her.

"You two know each other before Poppy moved here?" Heavy asked.

"Nope," I answered the nosy bastard knowing exactly what he was getting at. I had just claimed another brother's woman in front of him and he wanted to know if I was part of the reason she was here instead of there working shit out with him. I was sure rumors would start flying, if they hadn't already, but I didn't really want to stand there and hash it all out while Poppy had to deal with it. I just wanted to spend a good day with my woman. "I'll catch up with you guys later. We need to go deliver these cookies Poppy made."

"I'll grab the door for you." Crutch moved to do just that. The guy had been patched over long before I moved from Sierra High to Cedar Falls, but I swear I don't know how he earned it. The man was all manners and proper speaking. He rarely used what I'm sure his mom would consider foul language. He loved bikes though, and he had a great head for business which was honestly the reason I think he was patched in. We needed well-rounded riders to keep the club successful, even if they didn't always fit the mold.

"Thanks, man," I tipped my chin up to him as we passed through the door and then I heard it. It was as if he'd been waiting and watching for me to show. "Unc Moke!" I grinned at my nephew as he ran up and clung to my lower leg. I moved my arm from around Poppy's shoulders where I had used it to guide her through the door with me, and I patted his head. As usual, Brantley wrapped himself completely around my leg, signaling he was coming along for the ride whether I liked it or not. I moved toward the bar so we could stash the goodies Poppy had made and pretended that I didn't even know I had extra weight I was carrying around all of a sudden.

Then I took Poppy's bag from her and tossed it on the counter too before I snagged my nephew up and tossed him in the air declaring, "No free rides!" Then I proceeded to introduce my nephew to my girl, and shit you not, the little fucker was hitting on my woman telling me how pretty she was.

Before the little brat could start asking her out on a date for milk and cookies, I cut in. "Brantley," I addressed him so that Poppy would know his actual name and not the bastardized version of it that Brant said since he couldn't pronounce it right yet. "Where's your mom?" He pointed and my eyes followed the direction to see my sister was with her husband across the room. "Why don't you go ask your mom if you can have a cookie. I think Poppy made a special one just for you, bud."

"You did?" he asked in surprise.

"I did, but you can only have it once your mommy says it's okay."

"Momma!" I put the kid down and he was off and running after screaming to get Soph's attention. "Popwee made me spetial cookies! Can I eats them?"

I had to hope that my sister acted right today. If I could cross my fingers in the way of old superstitions and get away with not being seen by anyone else doing it, I would have. Knowing my sister, the day was not going to go by without her inserting her opinion at some point. 'Just not at the beginning of the day!' It was like a chant in my head repeating in a hurried cadence while Poppy took the time to

54

unpack the special cookie before we managed to make our way over to where my sister and Bender were standing. Soph did not appear happy to see us, and the chant in my head quickly deflated and died as we approached. This was probably going to happen. I glanced around to see if Chief was here yet, because if my sister insulted Poppy, there was no way he was going to let it go uncensured. Not that I would want him to.

Brantley helped cut the tension a little when he spoke up. "Momma, can I haz a spetial cookie pweeeez?" Bender laughed before offering up an apologetic look. He knew what was about to happen too. Fuck. I was about to just grab Poppy's arm and pull her away before shit could go down, but then she was talking, and being so sweet. I had a moment's worth of hope that my sister would see how genuine she was and keep her mouth shut.

"Whenever you're ready for him to have that," She offered as she held the special cookie out that she had made for my nephew. Then she smiled at Bender as he addressed her and held his hand out to shake.

"We already met when you moved in, but I'm Bender. This is my old lady, and Smoke's sister, Sophie. This little guy is Brantley."

"Thanks again for helping move me in," Poppy told him before turning her attention to my sister. "I'm Poppy." My sister was pulling a bitch card and didn't bother taking her hand like Bender had. "I'm Chief's sister," my woman added, in case there was any confusion. Bender and I both stared at Soph, willing her to behave.

"Sorry," Soph finally spoke, and I just knew she was

pulling her shit together and was going to act right. "I was just confused by you showing up with my brother since you're married and all." Then again, I had been wrong about Soph before.

"Are you fuckin' kidding me, Soph?" I asked my sister through clenched teeth, about to rip her a new one right there, until I felt a small hand clamped down around my arm and took in the delicate shake of Poppy's head. She didn't want this scene to play out here where everyone was tuning in to the drama. I reigned in my anger and let her handle the situation since that was what she seemed to be asking me to do.

"I am still married. I'm in the middle of a divorce at the moment and, while I would love that it was all over already, my ex is being a pain in the butt and trying to stall in order to get money for the sale of my family's home and lands." She offered up her business to my sister even though she didn't have to and I was both proud of the way she was handling it and embarrassed that she had to stand here spilling her dirty laundry where anyone could hear because my sister was being an asshole.

"He's a brother in the club," Soph managed to get out. The message clear, even in her hushed tone.

"Yes, he's with the Sierra High Chapter," Poppy explained needlessly.

"Why would he need your family's money?" Soph asked, not understanding.

Poppy's shoulders hitched up and down. "I don't begin to understand anything Walker does, so I couldn't tell you. If you'll excuse me, I'm going to see if my brother's around yet," and with that, my woman was making it clear she'd had enough of my sister.

"Poppy," I called out to her as she started walking away. "I'll be right behind you in a minute. Chief's at the pool tables." I'd clocked him walking in, just before Soph started in on Poppy. Once I thought my woman was far enough away, I turned back to my sister, not willing to spare her feelings since she had been more than okay with putting Poppy on blast the way she had. "What the fuck is your problem?"

"I – I don't know," she admitted. "I don't like that you're with her, or that she decided to latch on like a fucking leech the minute she got in town," my sister hissed, her brief moment of feeling guilty quickly forgotten.

I grabbed hold of her arm and yanked her further into the corner away from prying eyes and Bender took the cue, moving Brantley to the bar to eat his cookie. "Let me clue you in, little sister. Not that you deserve to know shit about my life or the decisions I make considering how you just behaved, but Poppy didn't latch onto me. It was the other way around. The minute I met her; I knew. I knew she would be the one to rock my fucking world, and I wasn't wrong. Neither of us can help the timing of when we met, but I promise you this, if we had met when we did, or five days from then, a year, or even a decade later, the results would have been the same. Never in my life felt a pull like that to another human being on this planet, and then when we talked, and everything just clicked into place like we'd been doing it for our whole lives – hell, maybe longer – I knew I wouldn't be letting her go. Even when she was skittish and gave me the 'it's too soon, let's just be friends speech.' So, you wanna get up on your high horse about someone being a leech and not showing signs of letting go, then you better point that accusing finger of yours at me, and only me. If you're worried about Poppy still being married and me going after her anyway then you go stand in Chief's corner and start asking what my intentions are toward his sister. Because of me, she will face all kinds of scrutiny, and that ain't fair to her. Hell, you just proved how unfair it is, but I'm selfish enough to want to keep her in my life, and just pummel anyone who has anything bad to say about her or us."

"What are your intentions?" My sister asked cautiously.

"I intend to make her my woman, my family, and every-thing else along the way that you can think of. That fuck-wit in Georgia didn't appreciate what he was throwing away because she didn't belong to him, and he probably knew that all along."

My sister rolled her eyes at me. "They were married for what? Ten years, Smoke? You can't just make statements like that."

"I can, and I did, because it's the truth. A man knows. He knows when a woman is too good for him, not good enough, or the perfect fucking fit to the puzzle that is his life. She's my perfect fit, and I'd bet you anything he felt like she was always too good for him."

"That doesn't say much for her," my sister offered snidely with a wrinkled nose.

"You mistake that shit, Soph. I don't mean she felt that way. I mean he did, and that's why his insecure ass was off looking at other ass. He was waiting for the ball to drop and her to get wise and leave him." I pointed to her husband who was watching us warily from across the room still. "That man there, he knew you were his perfect fit. He snatched you up, and to this day, you can still see it in the sap's eyes when he watches you. Even when you're being a bitch who is completely out of line, he still thinks you're his perfect piece that completes his puzzle."

Her lip wobbled a bit and I knew I'd made my point. "You really feel that strongly about her? It hasn't been that long."

"How long before you knew Bender was it for you?"

She glanced over at her husband and smiled. "I knew I was going to marry that man the first time we were introduced." She laughed then. "Long before he knew it."

"I should fuckin' hope so!" Bender was a few years older than me and they had met for the first time when I brought my sister and brother around to a club family cookout just after I was patched in. She was still in high school then and not even legal. He had to be about 24 or 25 at the time. "There's a goddamn 10-year age gap between you."

She waved that off. "More like nine and a half," she argued.

"Anyway," I attempted to redirect her.

"Yeah, I know. I get your point. I'm sorry, okay?"

"No, it's not. You just embarrassed her, and she was already insecure about how everyone here would treat her since she's already gone through becoming a pariah back in her hometown. Not to mention that you're my sister, and it has to make her feel even worse about just being my friend, let alone anything else right now, considering my own family jumped her shit about all the things that have been plaguing her."

"I said I was sorry," Sophie countered again.

"Yeah, but you're saying it to the wrong fuckin' person."

I walked away from my sister then, more than a little disappointed in her. She'd never been blatantly mean to people that I'd seen before, but the way she had treated Poppy was unacceptable. I attempted to shake it off and went to the bar to nab a beer before I headed over to where Poppy was hanging out with her brother by the pool table. By the time I got to her, half of my beer was gone and I had managed to shake off or bury most of the residual anger I was carrying. That shit didn't belong to Poppy, and I didn't want to run the risk of it coming out in front of her. I just had to hope that Poppy was going to behave better than my sister had. If she didn't, I couldn't blame her though.

"Food's up out back. You want to go grab something?" I asked before reaching out and taking her hand in my own. I didn't know what it was about the woman. I hadn't been very handsy with Julie when we were together. Sure, we touched, but we never really did the hand holding shit. I used to think that was too high school to bother with. Now, I was starting to see that it just meant that you enjoyed another person you couldn't help but try to be connected to them in every way possible.

Once we got outside, I slowed, giving Poppy a chance to take everything in. She seemed to be soaking in the glorious-ness of the multi-tiered decking we had built out here as well as looking to see where she might need to fill a space. I never thought about it before coming here tonight. She wasn't my old lady, because she couldn't be right now. She also wasn't here as Walker's old lady or even Smoke's sister. Poppy was the girl I brought along with me. Considering the hierarchy of women around a clubhouse, it had to be confusing to her as to where she fit in. I pulled her over toward the food thinking we'd just grab some plates, have a seat, and relax when Jewel sashayed her ass my way.

"This your new woman?" she asked in a snide tone I didn't much appreciate. I would have thought Phoenix, our lone-wolf nomadic brother who claimed her, would get her shit under wraps at some point but he didn't seem to be having much luck. She still dressed like she was trying out for best club whore of the year with part of her boobs visible. I wasn't one to judge, and maybe he liked his woman showing her body to everyone, but had Poppy been here with half her tits hanging out the bottom of her shirt I'd have her in a room, over my knee, showing her what happens to bad girls who don't know how to behave.

The worst part of Jewel's approach was the very visible snub she was giving Poppy by not even acknowledging her. "Poppy is my woman. She's also Chief's sister," I informed her while offering up a bit of glare that told her she was treading on thin ice. "Be nice, or we'll have problems. Don't care who your dad or your man is now."

Jewel was brought into the club as a whore to service the men. The problem with that was she refused to do the older guys. If they were above 38 or so, she wouldn't touch them. All hell broke loose when the club confronted her, threatened to boot her out on her ass, and she spilled the beans. Her mother had once been a club whore for Aces High MC too back in the day. She'd managed to get herself knocked up, and instead of using it to anchor the brother to herself, she fled without telling anyone they might have become daddy. Then, her crazy-as-fuck mother sent her to work the same job in a clubhouse where her own father might end up.

I shivered just thinking about it. At least her mom had been kind enough to tell her to avoid the older men at all costs. The woman was evil incarnate, using Jewel's position to try to help clear her drug debt. Bitch ended up dead, the secret came out, and now Jewel had both a father and an old man out of the situation. Hopper drew the straw on fatherhood while Phoenix ended up seeing something in her damaged soul that appealed to him. He claimed her, and they only rarely came around the clubhouse since he was nomad and they traveled a lot.

"Don't mind her," Cindy – Hopper's old lady – was telling Poppy after Jewel walked away. "That one has always had a bad attitude. She didn't grow up in the club thanks to her no-good momma. Didn't have much of a good influence for the same reason, so make no mind." Cindy held out her hand. "I believe we actually met a few years ago when you came up for an event. I'm Cindy, Hopper's old lady."

The rest of the afternoon went pretty much the same way. People remembered Poppy, even though she hadn't been around here much before. It seemed for those people she had interacted with previously, she managed to leave a big impression – most of all on Ghost who stole her sweet rib recipe. Sophie played nice after her, Brant, and Bender came to sit with us at a table and, finally, things were feeling good. I hated my family being at odds. I'd had that drama with my brother over the Julie situation for years. I didn't want to live with it again. Then again, I didn't want to lose Poppy over my sister's inability to separate rumor, gossip, and reality.

Thankfully, that wasn't the case and by the time we all went our separate ways that night the two had been getting along, and it seemed something Poppy had said to my sister changed how Soph saw things, even if only a little.

7. NOTHING BUT ICE

G**HOST AND** L**EANNE OFFERED TO WATCH** B**UBBA FOR** P**OPPY SO THAT** I could finally take her back to Pittsburgh to meet my brother. This time we were going to get more than five minutes with him before he had to run off to do whatever it was that was more important than us the last time we'd come up. At least this time, we were hanging out at his house so we wouldn't have to deal with the puck bunnies like we had last time. My brother being in the NHL could be a pain the ass from time to time since there were always eyes on him. Everyone wanted a piece of him, and my ex had been no exception. I wondered briefly if Poppy would turn out to be the same since she was such a huge fan. I had purposely avoided telling her much about Julie and the reason we split just to see how things played out. It sounded bad, thinking about it in my head that way, but shit was what it was. I would be an idiot to say I wasn't the tiniest bit worried.

It turned out, I had absolutely nothing to worry about. "That slap shot in the third period was a thing of beauty!"

Poppy praised my brother as we all walked up to his apartment after the game.

Kent grinned at my woman before turning to me. "How the hell did you end up with the hot chick who actually knows hockey, and isn't a fuckin' bunny?"

I cringed inwardly knowing that he considered Julie nothing more than a puck bunny who didn't actually know all that much about hockey and, instead, faked it with him in the hopes of getting him to accept his offer. "You get to play, brother, that's all the reward you're getting. Leaves time for me to snatch up Poppy for myself."

The woman blessed me with one of her full smiles that made the skin around her eyes crinkle ever so slightly as she did. I thought I heard my brother mumble something like, "fuckin' sap" under his breath, but I was honestly too taken in by Poppy to care.

"Of course, you did manage to eat ice right after that slap shot though," Chief pointed out.

My brother rubbed his jaw, but grinned as he did it. "Worth it since we won though," he chimed in. The guys continued talking about sports as Poppy and I watched one another. Every now and again, one of them would draw her into the conversation and I'd just take it all in and watch as she interacted with men I considered to be my brothers in different ways. One brother by blood, one by club, and the other one because our job was life and death and it formed the same type of bond between us. She managed to work her magic over the each of them every time she spoke. Even as she gave them all her attention, she never strayed far from me, her eyes always drifted back to check in with me and give a smile of contentment or reassurance. I wasn't sure which, maybe a bit of both, but I liked that she thought to do it. For the first time in years, it felt good to settle into my brother's ugly ass apartment.

That was all before I got the call from the club though. My phone went off at the same time that Chief's did which could only signal bad things. "Yeah?" I asked

"I know you and Chief are both off in Pittsburgh, but we need you for a while."

"Me specifically, or the two of us because you need numbers?"

"You specifically," Ghost informed me.

"Fire?"

"You could say that. I'm texting the address. Closer to you guys than to us. Don't suppose any of you took a cage so that Poppy can get back on her own?"

"Sure as fuck didn't," I huffed out knowing what this was going to mean. I glanced over at Chief who had furrowed brows scrunched down as he read something on his phone. "I'll figure something out," I told him before I hung up. There was no way I could take Poppy with us, which meant Chief couldn't either. We were about to handle club business and if they needed my skill set, that meant it was nothing good and nothing we needed to expose my woman to. I stood and moved with Chief to the other room momentarily.

"You going to be okay with her staying here without us?" I asked Chief. His face was turning a darker shade of his normal deeply tanned skin and his head was shaking back and forth in a negative response, though I wasn't sure he was consciously doing it.

"You know I'm not. I like Kent and Shep, but that don't mean shit. They're both strangers to her."

"What the fuck am I supposed to do here?"

He huffed out a breath. "I don't know. I get the fact that we don't have much of a choice, but I don't fuckin' like it."

"That makes two of us then," I agreed. When we explained to the others that we had to go because there was a club emergency, I could have punched my brother and hugged Poppy for their responses. Despite my urging that we shouldn't be held up too long, my brother looked both pissed and disappointed in me. Poppy was the opposite. She accepted the fact that we had club business and had to go, and she assured both Chief and me that she would be just fine, even if that meant getting a ride back with someone else. Fuck, that woman! I didn't think there was a better one out there for me anywhere, which made leaving her behind that much more difficult.

The absolute last thing I wanted to do was have to leave Poppy with my brother and Shep in Pittsburgh. Not that I didn't trust any of them, but I didn't know if Poppy would hate me for doing it. She didn't really know either of them and there she was basically stuck, because I'd taken the bike she rode to town on. I'd actually never left a woman behind out of town like that before and it rankled that I had to do it now. Granted, there was the one exception – Julie – but when I left her, I never went back. Now I had to hope that Poppy wouldn't decide to get home and never look back too.

It didn't help my guilt any that Chief was beyond pissed off with me and the decision to leave her there. The only alternative was to take her with us to a situation we weren't entirely sure about. The club called. They needed us, me and my skillset specifically, but what they didn't need was an old lady stuck in the mix too when club business was going down.

THE BIG CLUB emergency was actually at a warehouse we still maintained near the northeast border of West Virginia in the little strip of the state that stood between Ohio and Pennsylvania. It only took us a little under an hour to ride from the condo my brother had near the PPG Paints Arena to get to Hancock County and the ten acre tract of land we had just on the outskirts of New Manchester. There was nothing there beyond some old barns that we'd restored only on the inside to accommodate whatever we needed. We purposely left the exterior looking rundown so that we wouldn't have people nosing around them.

I saw the smoke long before we arrived, but hoped it wasn't the barns. As we pulled onto the land and rode down the dirt path that served as a driveway to the barns, any hopes I'd had were dashed. Two of the three barns on the property had been engulfed and were now in the controlled burn stage. The third barn had scorch marks on the outside like someone had attempted to set fire to it, but for some reason it didn't actually catch. I'd have to check that building thoroughly before leaving here to see what happened and why it hadn't gone up like the other two tinderboxes had. Granted, it wasn't what was above ground on any of the buildings that would matter. Everything of importance was held in secret bunkers we had installed beneath the structures. As long as they hadn't been compromised prior to the fire everything should still be safe inside.

Glancing around the scene, I knew that could end up being a problem for the club since there were so many police and firefighters on the scene. "Smoke," one of the officers tipped his head towards me as I dismounted my bike.

I glanced at the damaged, still burning buildings and shook my head. "What the hell?"

"That's what we're trying to figure out," the officer stated, causing me to turn my attention back to him.

"Scott," I replied as I tipped my chin up to the man who I'd gotten to know over the years. We spent a good deal of time up here when we were getting the place set up so we got to know a few of the locals rather well, including Jacob Scott, who I noticed was no longer simply a police officer. He appeared to be a plain clothed detective now. "You got a promotion?"

He grinned at me and answered with a nod. "Do I even want to know what you guys had going on in there?"

I lifted a shoulder suggesting my feigned indifference. "We rehabbed the insides a while back, as you know. Fitted everything out to be a clubhouse and bunkhouse," I stated as I pointed to the two buildings that were still burning. "Then the shed for bikes and part storage over there. We just hadn't gotten around to moving people around to start another chapter here yet."

"Quite a long time to just have freshly rehabbed barns

sitting empty isn't it? Seems like that would be a hefty loss if you weren't using the place as intended."

"Our club isn't hurting for cash. We have many lucrative businesses all over the country, man. Having this place sit until we needed it was no big deal. Honestly, I was supposed to move up this way in order to be closer to my brother, but shit happened. A woman held me up, and turned out not to be worthy after all. You know the drill."

He chuckled then. "Don't I know it. My wife took off a couple months after I made detective. She's shacked up with that asshole over there," he tipped his chin in the direction of a firefighter on scene. I raised my brows at him. "Fucking firefighters!" He hissed out playfully as he smacked my shoulder.

"Want me to have a word with him about the code?" There wasn't really much of a code where the woman of another cop, fire, or rescue personnel was concerned. Sure, it was a dick move to go after one, but they weren't as tight as the MC brotherhood in that way.

"Nah, he can have her. She spent more of my money than she was worth. Besides, I wanted a family and she wasn't interested in giving one to me." He waved off the thought. "Better it happened now than down the road when I should be a grandparent and still looking to try to have kids with someone, you know?"

I couldn't argue that, because the sentiment hit a little close to home for me. I had allowed Julie to take up residence too long in my life, and I might miss out on having a family of my own one day as a result. Then again, my thoughts turned to Poppy, and her desire to have children, and I smiled because it didn't seem too late for me after all. Not that being in my thirties was too late to start with a family, but I damn sure wasn't getting any younger.

"What do you need from us?" I finally asked him and waited as he stood around.

"Access," he informed me.

"Well, there's not a whole lot to gain access to now."

He smirked at me. "Come on now, we both know better than that." He turned to look toward the third barn that was still standing. "It'd be interesting to find out why that one wasn't burned to the ground too, don't you think?"

I shrugged. "Could be someone happened along the place and scared the assholes off."

"You guys are out here in the middle of nowhere," Scott countered.

"Okay, could be one of our guys came running out here as soon as we saw that someone was dicking around the place. We do still have security running here, as we do with all of our properties."

"I'd like to get a hold of that footage."

"Not saying there's any footage to get a hold of, Scott. I'm just speculating on some theories for why one of our buildings was spared. I just got here myself, so who knows?" I shrugged my shoulders again and then wandered away from him and toward the men who were still working on putting out the fire on the first two buildings.

"Chief Jones?" I asked one of the men, looking for the fire chief.

"Not here, far as I know. Deputy Chief Womack is just over there," he nodded his head in the direction of one of the responding engines and I moved to head that way. Deputy Chief Womack should be running the joint since Jones never bothered to show as a fire line officer to any fire event. He was also the man who had attempted numerous times to recruit me for their local station. I had been tempted. What I had told Detective Scott hadn't been a lie. We had considered opening a small chapter here due to its proximity to Pittsburgh, but the push hadn't been big enough at the time, so we decided to wait it out. That had been three years ago. In my mind, fate must have intervened because had I gone then, and started a chapter here, I never would have met Poppy. At least, I wouldn't have met her in a way that would lead to whatever it was we were becoming.

By the time I located Womack, he looked fit to be tied. "Fucking idiots, I tell you. Why the hell couldn't I convince you to come and work for me here?" I asked before he ever turned around to see that it was me standing behind him. The man had eyes in the back of his head.

"Well, if I had been here, I may have gone down with those buildings," I suggested. He simply laughed at my theory.

"No, you fucking wouldn't have because you're not a dumbass. You want to tell me what's really going on here?"

"No clue," I told him honestly. "That's what I'm here to find out. Looked like scorch marks on the third barn, but it didn't burn. That's probably a big clue."

"You seriously have no idea what could have happened here tonight?" he asked as he finally turned to give me his full attention.

"None. I was over in Pittsburgh introducing my woman

to Kent. Hell, I just introduced them and had to leave her there with him in order to haul ass over here to see what the hell was going on."

"Well shit. I was hoping you'd be able to shed some light. Not that I thought it would be in an official capacity since you wear the leather, but you know I hate unsolved puzzles."

I grinned at the man then. In another life, he probably would have made a good brother. The problem was, the man hated motorcycles. His younger brother died while messing around on one when they were kids, and he hasn't been able to look at them the same since. It was a discussion we had when he was actively attempting to recruit me to work for him.

"No known enemies? Anyone the club pissed off lately?" He started to rattle off questions. For the first time in a lot of years, I could honestly say that there wasn't really anything like that going on. Granted, there was the issue recently with the Hell's Hounds trying to move in on the guns our guys out of Tallahassee were running, but that was typical club shit. We didn't store guns up here. The guns came to us out of a little town south of Chicago and we helped get them transported safely to our meet point with the Florida guys. Not once did we ever stop near this property on those runs. That couldn't be what this had been about.

"I can't even remember the last time one of our men was up here," I started to tell him and then it hit me. I knew exactly when the last time someone had been here was. When we helped Shep's family out, I brought the women here to stay for a couple days until he could get them set up with a solid place to stay since his apartment was only an open plan studio. I did my best to keep the thought from showing in my face. "Keep me in the loop on what you find in there, yeah?"

He slapped my shoulder. "You know I will, son. Damn shame this happened. You think you guys will rebuild them or finally let this place go?" His words were solemn as he waited for the news of whether he'd be seeing me around again after this.

"I'm not sure. I'm going to check in with Ghost and let him know what's up so far. We'll have a better idea of where to go in the future once we find out what exactly happened here."

"You do that, and Smoke?" He glanced back at me once more before I could walk away. "Try to keep me in the loop too. I was really rooting for you boys to move in up here. Hell, if Travis were still alive, he'd have been all over himself trying to prospect for you."

I smiled at the man. "That would have made us family, because I have no doubt he'd have been an asset if he was anything like you." I meant it too. "I'll check with you before you take off, Womack."

He nodded and then went back to looking over something on the laptop he had with him. I made sure to walk off to a more secure area before I put the call in to Ghost.

"Talk to me," he answered.

"Two barns down, the third smaller one is still standing despite scorch marks where someone attempted to take it out too and didn't have time to make sure the fire caught."

"Any clue as to who the fuck managed to do get most of the job done?"

"Not yet, but I'm developing a theory. We brought Shep's mom and sister here after we got them away."

"Okay, I'll have the guys run the info. You want to give Shep a call?"

"Not yet," I explained as I looked up and noticed Chief headed my way. "Looks like Chief has something to add. I'm going to gather more intel and get back to you. Seems the only plausible theory we have right now though.

"Keep me posted, and Smoke?"

"Yeah?"

"If this is because of our involvement with Shep's situation, I do not want you carrying that weight on your shoulders."

"You know better," I told him as I hung up. Sure, I'd feel bad because ultimately it was me that dragged the club into Shep's situation, but I would do it all over again because there was no way I would leave Shep's mom and sister to suffer the fate that awaited them had we not stepped in. They were both about to become nothing more than sex slaves to pay off his step-father's debt. There wasn't a man in our club who wouldn't step in and make sure that never happened.

"What do you have?" I asked Chief as he came up on my side.

"Was that Ghost?" I nodded. "Well, it looks like we had some visitors that maybe we have seen around before."

"You tapped into the security feed from here?"

"Yeah, but just the one we hid in the tree line," he tipped his head toward where we had a camera hidden in the trees just in case the ones by the building were ever compromised.

"Got a good look at a white cargo van that was in here. Looks like the stormed through the buildings looking for something, and didn't find what they wanted to. They left empty handed and came back to torch the place. I have some half-ass decent images of the two assholes who were doing the dirty work. One of them I recognized."

"When we helped Shep?"

"Yeah, it was one of the goons we found watching the house there." Chief sighed before going on. "It's looking like these guys have some sort of mob connection or something, man. I'm not sure what Ghost is going to want to do, but I think Shep needs to consider getting his family gone from the area. If these assholes were able to find where we stashed the girls for a few days they will, no doubt, find them back in Cedar Falls."

"I'll let him know." Before we could manage anything else, the ground beneath our feet shook as the third barn went up in a blazing inferno. The heat from the blast actually reached us even though we were far enough away that we hadn't been able to feel the radiating warmth from the other fires. Yelling, and movement of the men attending the fires bled into the chaos that surrounded us after the barn went up. I glanced at Chief and then back into the scattering bodies.

"Mother fucker!" I heard Womack growl out into the night. "Who went in?"

Two names were called out and immediately my stomach plummeted. "Jesus fuck! The department just lost two of their own. They aren't gonna be able to let this investigation slide one bit now," I commented quickly to Chief.

"Call Ghost, fill him in. The third barn was rigged. The scorch marks were probably there for appearances so we wouldn't think about what was waiting for us inside there."

Chief shook his head in disbelief. "What the fuck were they doing going inside there anyway?"

"I don't know, but I'm about to find out." I tipped my chin to Womack who was storming my way.

"You want to tell me what you know now? Two of my men might not make it after that blast!" Womack's seething shouts were not unexpected. Still, it was obvious I'd already been cooperating.

"We don't know any more than you do. Besides, your men should have known better than to go charging into a building that hadn't been secured yet considering foul play was expected here," I informed him of something he already knew. Then I poked a finger toward the building that was now nothing more than timber and flame consuming everything around the steel vault that had been placed inside it. "You saw the fucking scorch marks. Whoever did this gave your guys a fucking warning that none of them heeded. Did you see my ass storming in my own fucking building to check on things? No, because I knew it hadn't been cleared yet!" I screamed back at the man. I was just as angry over his men's fuck up as he was. I wouldn't be his whipping boy though. "They probably just single-handedly got rid of the evidence we needed to collect in order to find out for sure who did this."

Womack snatched the cap he wore off his head and threw it with the might of a man who just found out he had the whole world resting on his shoulders. "I want the fucking surveillance tapes you guys have. We want a crack at whoever was responsible for this too."

I gave him a nod, though I refused to give him a promise because depending on how the club handled this situation, it might become incriminating for us to do so. "I'll do what I can, but no telling when the feeds were killed. If they were tampered with before the fires, or what."

He crewed his eyes up tight, lips pulled to thin lines on his craggy face as he took a deep breath in and then let it out again. "Do your best, Smoke, but make no mistake I will not let this one simply rest. Those are my men," he explained pointing his hand in the direction of where two men were being placed on stretchers to be taken to the nearest trauma center.

"We'll make sure their expenses are seen to," I told him. It was the least we could do as a club since they were hurt on our property trying to help us out.

"Fat lot of good that's going to do them if they don't make it."

What could I say to that? Nothing. He didn't give me a moment to attempt to placate him either. Womack walked away heading in the direction of the rescue squads that were heading out with the men who had been injured. "This is a cluster fuck of epic proportions," Chief mentioned.

"Did you let Ghost know what just happened?"

"Yeah, I did. He wants us both to stay put long enough for you to be able to get in there once the flames are out. He wants answers, but he also wants everything we have underground kept secure until he can get the rest of the guys up here to pull it all out."

"Fuck," I growled out. "I need to call Shep and Kent."

"Don't you mean you need to call Poppy?"

"I need to talk to them first and see what they're willing to do for her. If they can't get her home safely, then I will have to call one of the club women to run up there with a prospect or something." I mumbled as I was basically thinking out loud.

"Get to it then. I'm sure my sister is worried, and not to mention she's been left with two men she hardly knows."

"You know," I told him as I threw my hand up to indicate the mess we were standing in the middle of. "I didn't exactly have a choice."

"I fucking know, and it still pisses me off, so deal with it."

8. LOSSES

ONE THING AFTER ANOTHER WAS BOUND AND DETERMINED TO KEEP me from getting back to Poppy. I finally had to ask Kent and Shep to make sure she got home okay, and it killed me to do it. Hell, Chief nearly killed me for having to make that call too. At least, he threatened it until I pointed out that he wasn't exactly in a position to go back for her either.

"We need to call a lock down," I suggested to Ghost when I finally got some information and had to call him back. "I've already let Shep know that his family needs to remain hidden for a while, but I think these fuckers are going to keep coming at us until we produce them."

"What the fuck kind of shit was his step-dad into?"

"The mafia, for a few large apparently. I think one of them was looking forward to having Shep's sister as payment though." I swore when I glanced down at what looked like a human remain sitting at my feet outside the barn. The locals had missed something here after the explosion. I didn't know what to do with that sight and ended up staring at the digit that sat in the dirt near the toe of my well-worn leather boot. "They aren't afraid of making a statement considering they just took out a few cops with the explosion they had rigged. Either they thought we'd go charging in our own building, or they were purposely trying to turn the heat up for us with the law."

"Either way, I think you're right. I just sent out a lock-down notice to everyone."

"What about Poppy?"

I could almost hear the smile in Ghost's voice when he answered. "Leanne went to get her."

"You have someone on Leanne?"

"Of fucking course, I have someone on Leanne. I ain't sending my woman out there unprotected."

"Soph, Bender, and Brant?" I asked after the rest of my family.

"Haven't been able to get a hold of them. Bender mentioned them taking a short trip earlier today though." He sighed. "Been trying to call them back, but you know Bender. They go on their little family excursions and he doesn't answer shit."

"Yeah, sometimes hate the fucker for that, but I'm Soph's brother too, so I have to love the fact that he's putting them first."

"We'll keep trying to get a hold of them. I've put 911 texts in to both of their phones in case they turn them back on."

"Appreciate it, brother."

"Get me something we can use," Ghost demanded.

"Working on it." It wasn't a lie, but there wasn't a fuck of a lot to go on since most of the evidence had been blown to smithereens, and what was left had been collected by the cops and then trampled over by the fire department as they too went through looking for anything the cops left behind.

"Anything?" Chief asked as he moved closer to me, noticing the thumb that I had been staring at on the ground. "Jesus! You'd think they would have at least made sure to get all of their men's parts."

I shrugged my shoulders. "They're too close."

"Yeah, that's why shit's gonna end up fucked," Chief muttered. He wasn't wrong either. It was already showing in their sloppy collection activity.

"Leanne is taking Poppy into lockdown with her," I informed him since he was her brother.

"Good." He sighed heavily then. "Heard some shit from Snake before that never sat right with me." I turned to watch as he tried to reel his anger in. "When the men in Georgia were dealing with the human trafficking ring, the fucking third wave of those fuckers coming into their territory trying to fuck with their shit, Poppy was left home alone in a farm-house that had no fuckin' protection. Bastard didn't tell me until after the fact."

"What the fuck?"

"Probably making sure the club whores didn't whisper anything in her ear about his habits."

"Motherfucker!" I snapped. "It's getting past time we took a ride to Georgia to straighten this fucker out."

"Nope," Chief disagreed.

"What the fuck do you mean by nope?"

"He'll get what's coming to him, but you have to keep your hands clean. Poppy wouldn't want that. She wouldn't want the drama of club brothers going at each other and causing strife. Trust me on that. Hell, she's better to the club than that particular chapter deserves, but I promise you, she'll be pissed if you do anything against Walker."

"I feel like my hands are tied behind my back and I'm walking this tight rope blindfolded."

"I know it, brother. Let everything sort itself and settle. Then, we'll have a come to Jesus meeting with the asshole who couldn't take care of my sister properly. I promise you. It's coming." He tipped his chin down towards the digit that was still taunting me. Something about it set me off and it didn't settle in until that moment. "Let's get this shit to the cops.

"Nah, we're not gonna do that."

"Why the fuck not?"

"This little digit doesn't belong to them. Check out that ring. Know many cops that wear a pinky ring?"

Chief leaned in to take a better look. "Holy fuck. One of those bastards blew himself up?"

"Looks like it. Must have come from the initial blaze or explosion." I pulled a knife from my belt and knelt to stab the thumb. Then I brought it up closer to my face to check out the jewelry on the damn thing just a little closer. The ring was a golden revolver cylinder with one chamber filled and topped with what looked like a ruby. There was also a partial tattoo present at the base of the thumb where it would have connected to the index finger.

"You know what that is?"

I nodded my head. "I do because a guy that used to run with the club for a while back when I was prospecting had one. VTK. It's Russian and used to indicate that the person was in a labor camp before they were 18. It's a youth offender designation."

"Think it's the same guy you knew from back then?"

"No. Couldn't be. He fucking died in a fire, of all things, not too long after I met him. The bastard was shacked up in a crack den that burned to the damn ground with him and two others in it."

"You sure about that?"

The more I stared at the ink on the thumb, the more my worry became a real thing. These people weren't ones to be trifled with. We had a huge club with a shitload of chapters throughout the country, but we were also a club on the cusp of trying to go filly legit. Throwing down with the Russian Mafia could derail those plans exponentially, especially if the outcome – like buildings blowing up cops – put us on the radar of the feds. Our guys in Tallahassee were almost free of their gun running responsibilities they had to pick up ten years back as a result of a deal they needed to make in order to get rid of some corrupt ass government officials and their family who had been terrorizing the area and the chapter's president's old lady.

"I'm sure enough to know we should all probably be shaking in our boots."

"You don't think we can take them?"

"It's not about that. We have to worry about how deep the fallout will roll, how many people will end up dead in the wake, and how many eyes we have on us just as we're pulling out of the last of the shit that keeps us dirty."

"Well, fuck!" Chief hissed out as he walked off again and

raised his cell back to his ear, speaking to someone on the other end.

We were just about to leave when Womack pulled up on the scene his men had torn apart the day before. He didn't bother getting out of his vehicle, just rolled the window down and handed me a large brown envelope. "Not so sure I should be doing this, but it's in my head that you boys wouldn't bring this sort of attention down on yourselves. I have to think there's good reason for it." I nodded my head indicating that there was. "Thought that might be the case. That's everything we gathered so far. Catalogued it all, cops gave us their list, and we're working this jointly considering. Do what you need to with that information, but don't let it out of your sight because you'll never see it from me again. That's all the help I can give you boys." He tipped his head up and started to roll his window back up and thought better of it before turning back and sending a warning of his own. "Might want to tell Ghost to start lookin' for some new property. Think this site is just about used up all the welcome you boys were ever gonna get."

"It's been a pleasure, Womack," I called out.

"Wish I could say it ended the same, Smoke." With a shake of his head, and a swipe at his window control Womack cut himself off from us and took off back down the bumpy, unpaved road that brought him out here.

"Let's get this back," I suggested before tucking the envelope of papers into my saddlebags.

WE WERE HALFWAY home when my cell phone would not stop buzzing in my pocket. I finally got fed up and decided answering it was better than wondering what the hell had them calling me so frantically. "Yeah?" I asked into the receiver after pulling off the interstate.

"How close are you?" Ghost's gruff voice had the hairs on my arms standing on end.

"Halfway, why?"

"You need to get here as quick as you can brother and bypass the clubhouse. Get to the hospital."

"The hospital? Is Poppy okay?" Chief killed his engine and ran over when he heard his sister's name.

"She's fine. Asleep at the clubhouse still, last I saw her."

A horrible feeling sunk deep down in my stomach as I recalled Ghost telling me they had tried to pull Bender and my sister in for lockdown but had been unsuccessful in getting a hold of them. "Soph? Brant?" I asked.

"Get here!" He hung up.

"FUCK!" I screamed. "Fuck!"

"Calm down brother. We don't know what's happening just yet. Not gonna help anyone sitting here losing your shit. Let's get back and see what's up, okay?"

All I could do was nod, or losing my shit would be the least of our worries. I had this feeling. I wasn't going to get to say goodbye to my sister no matter how quickly I got there. I couldn't even allow myself to think about my innocent little nephew, or my club brother. What the fuck would I do if we lost them all? If we lost any of them? SHIT!

There should have been a bit over two hours left on our ride back. We made it back in half that.

9. BLACK AND BLUE

My heart hammered against my chest as I dove from my bike, not even able to remember if I'd snatched the keys out, because I was in too big a hurry to make it inside. "Sophie and Granger Bent?" I shouted. "Brantley Bent?"

Immediately sad, pitying eyes met my own and it stopped me short. "Sir,"

"I'm Sophie's brother, Brantley's Uncle," I explained.

"Smoke!" I turned to see Ghost standing there with a doctor and rushed toward them.

"What's going on?"

Ghost reached for me and immediately wrapped his arms around my shoulders, effectively tucking my hands between us. "Soph and Bender are gone, brother. Brantley's okay. They're just checking him out right now. He survived."

"What the fuck did he survive? What do you mean they're gone?"

"As I was explaining to Mr. Ghost here," some asshole

doc was saying before I turned around and he took note of who I was. Hell, I wasn't in and out of here as often as Surfer was, but enough that people knew me. "Oh, sorry, I didn't realize, Mr. Lewis."

"I've got it from here," Ghost informed him.

"We'll need you to sign for your nephew before he can be released since..." his voice trailed off as I stood there engulfed in Ghost's arms.

"I have you. We have you, Smoke. We'll get through this."

"Kent," I managed to choke out.

"Already got word to him. They're sending him back from California."

"Jesus, fuck! How did this happen? What the fuck happened?"

Ghost released his hold on me and we both collapsed into the uncomfortable chairs sitting there just inside a room I hadn't even realized we had moved in to. Chief was there with us now and he tucked my keys into my hands. Apparently, I had left them behind.

"It looks like they were run off the road on purpose. Reports came in to the police that a white work van was trying to run a car off the road. They were in the Mustang, and..."

He didn't have to say it. My sister's Mustang was a convertible. "They rolled?"

He tipped his head up and down one time. "Doc says neither of them suffered. Brantley still being so small is the only thing that saved him. That and the car seat."

I had no words. My sister was gone. My club brother who

became a brother-in-law was gone with her. Now, there would be their little boy to care for in their absence and I honestly didn't know if I was up for the job. How did you tell a kid they just lost both of their parents and you and his other uncle were all they had left?

"The roads were slick, and from the reports, the assholes in the van were relentless."

"It was a hit?" I heard Chief ask.

"Looks that way," Ghost returned.

Nothing. I had nothing for that. After what we found at the barns I knew that things were about to get ugly. I'd even mentioned earlier that we were looking at potential casualties and collateral damage that might draw the interest of agencies we didn't want poking around in our business. Never, in a million years, had I envisioned my own family as a part of the losses. I'd saved Shep's mother and sister at the expense of my own sister and club brother. How the fuck was I ever going to make that right?

"He was there," Ghost murmured, as if reading my mind. "Bender was there with you when you went to help Shep. He'd do it all over again if he were here right now, and you know it. Don't take that shit on your shoulders or put it on Shep's. We're going to find the assholes responsible, and we're going to take every last one of the fuckers out. That is a fucking promise."

"Gonna hold you to that one," I managed to get out before the grief hit and I lost my shit right there in the waiting room for all to see. I've never been a man prone to tears, but my little sister was more to me. In a way, I had become a surrogate father for her, and she'd become my own child. Our sibling relationship was vastly different from many people's since I had to step up and take of her and Kent. My baby girl, my sister, was gone and there was nothing on this Earth that could bring her back to me. We had hardly talked since that barbecue where we had shitty fucking words to say to one another. While Poppy and Soph had managed to pull it together in the end, my sister and I still hadn't really managed an opportunity to talk about things and make it right between us.

"How the hell do I tell Brant?" I asked everyone and no one all at once. "Where is Brant?" Panic set in then. Somewhere in this hospital was a little boy who was probably scared shitless and wondering where his parents were and here I was becoming a sniveling mess in a waiting room. How had he not been my first thought? Shit, I was already fucking up.

I stood just as Ghost did, and he put a hand on my shoulder to hold me still a moment longer. "It's okay. BigMac's been sitting with him."

BigMac was one of the older brothers who was barely around anymore because arthritis was taking his ability to ride. Still, the man had a heart of gold and doted on his grandchildren like they were the most precious things this world had to offer. Hell, the fat bastard took it upon himself to beef up for the position of Santa at the club's Christmas events every year. He was already pushing 350 at only 5 feet 10 inches, and he took it seriously, because he wasn't about to disappoint the kids. Even knowing that, I couldn't let another man sit in on my responsibility any longer. "I need to go to him."

"I know you do. How about you take a minute to process first, and then get yourself cleaned up before you go in there shocking the kid with just your appearance. Shit's about to be hard enough."

"Has anyone told him?"

"Nah, we figured either you or Kent would want to do that."

"I don't think either of us wants that particular honor," I mumbled.

Ghost clapped a hand on my shoulder and squeezed. "I know you don't. I'm going to call Leanne and update her."

"Don't tell Poppy just yet. Please, let her know. I think it's best if that comes from me or Chief too."

Ghost nodded his head and stepped aside only for Chief to take his place. "Anything you need, brother. Anything. I mean that."

"I know you do," I told him.

"You want one of us in there when you tell Brant?"

"Would you mind?" I asked. It wasn't that I was afraid of telling the kid, though I wished I didn't have to. My heart hammered disturbingly fast against the body restraining it as I thought about how I would be when everything sunk in for Brant. Having backup didn't seem like a bad plan.

We took two steps toward the doorway of the waiting area before I realized I had no clue where to go. Ghost had disappeared to make his phone call and Chief had come in with me. I knew there were others here but they had all made themselves scarce at some point. Probably when I had come apart and cried like a fucking baby in the arms of my club president. "Shit, brother, I don't know where he is."

"Come on, we'll go find out together," Chief walked beside me, nudging me a little to get me going until we made our way to the nurses' station. "This is Jared Lewis. His sister, brother-in-law and nephew were brought in tonight. We're looking for his nephew Brantley Bent."

The nurse at the desk offered up a sad smile before checking something in her computer. Then she nodded and stood. "I'll take you to him. It's time to check his vitals anyway," she stated without stopping her forward momentum. We followed along behind her to a room about halfway down the corridor. When the door opened, I stopped and took a deep breath. I could do this. I had to do this. There simply wasn't a choice.

"Unc Moke," a small little boy voice called out to me as soon as I managed to get out from behind the nurse.

"Hey, little man, how are you feeling?"

He poked out his bottom lip out a bit as he glanced between the nurse and BigMac. The side of his face was mottled in bruises making me want to kill the mother fucker responsible all over again. "I got hurted. The car spinned on the road and I boomed me head and hanged with my hair falling to the grass." It took everything in me to stifle the choked scream that threatened to come out. The car was upside down. The fucking convertible was upside down with my family inside it.

"You're a brave kiddo," BigMac told him while ruffling his hair to draw attention from me while I got myself together.

"Did momma and daddy gets hurts too?" Brantley finally asked as he turned back to me. Both the nurse and BigMac's sympathy-filled eyes found my own. Shit. The kid was throwing out all the hard punches without meaning to.

"They did, buddy." I moved to go sit on the side of his bed. I closed my eyes and remembered what it had been like to explain to my siblings that our mom was gone, and not coming back. They had been older. I'm not sure that made it easier. Soph had vowed that God had taken her so she wouldn't suffer anymore, and I knew as I got in touch with that memory that it was what she would want me to tell her son.

"Brant, your mom and dad were hurt really bad, and instead of letting that happen to them, God came and took them away to a better place," I tried explaining. When I saw his lip wobble, I knew it wasn't going to go well.

"God wanted me to be hurted?" he questioned.

"No, buddy. God thought you could handle it, and he knew you had more to do in this life. He couldn't take you just yet, but one day you'll get to go be with your mom and dad again, okay?"

"Tomowo?"

"It won't be tomorrow, little man. It'll be after you live a good long life. Your mommy and daddy want you to be able to grow up and have lots of fun first."

"But dey won't be hewe to see," he told me quietly.

"When you go with God, it's like magic buddy. They can still see you, even if you can't see them. They'll know."

"Do I has to dwibe cars and gets a job now?"

"What? No, buddy."

"But dats what happsens when you don't has a mom or dad no more. You all gwowd up." He sniffled through the words, hiccuping at the end.

I carefully pulled his little body to me in a hug as tears I didn't think he knew he was shedding trailed down his chubby little cheeks. "I'm gonna take care of you, little man. You can still be a kid for a while, yeah?"

"Unc Moke, don't weave me too, otay?"

"I won't buddy. I promise you, I won't."

"Don't wet God take you too." His sleepy voice trailed off at the end.

"I'll punch the fucker if he tries," I managed through gritted teeth. He giggled.

"You punch God?"

"Nobody is taking me from you, little man!" I told him, though what I really wanted to say was completely different. Damn right I'd punch God. That fucker had been taking from me for far too long now. If he had a plan, it fucking sucked, and I probably wouldn't be the only one standing in line waiting to sucker punch him either. It had been a long time since I believed though. Now, I'd only pretend for Brant's sake. When he grew older, he could decide for himself. Before I got to God though, there would be some Russian mafia fucks were about to pay the price for what they'd just done to my family. I couldn't tell Brant just yet that it wasn't God that took his family from him, but one day when he was old enough to ask questions and realize what happened, he would know that I managed swift fucking justice for them.

I gently leaned Brant back down on the bed once he had

fallen asleep in my arms. Then I pulled the chair BigMac had vacated closer to the bed and held his little hand in my own.

"I have to head out to the clubhouse to check on things there and-"

"Please, make sure Poppy knows I'm okay," I requested before he could finish his sentence.

"I will, brother. Is there anything you need before I leave?"

I shook my head. The only fucking thing I needed was for my sister and her husband not to be dead. I dropped my head down on the mattress of the bed beside where Brant's hand rested in my own. "Nothing you can bring me," I mumbled. I felt his hand on my shoulder as he squeezed.

"I'll be back as soon as I can. We'll have someone standing outside. Get some rest if you can. Holler if you need anything."

"Yeah," I managed to get out and before I knew it I drifted off into a sleep I didn't think would be possible.

THERE WAS no telling how long I'd managed to nod off before I felt another presence in the room. To explain the feeling was akin to holding a magnet close to iron. She drew me in and held on tight from the moment I met her, whether she intended for that to happen or not wasn't an issue, because we both felt the undeniable pull. I struggled to open my swollen eyes. I'd been crying in my sleep and knew it because the sheets beneath my face were soaked, and my eyes felt like their lids were made of sandpaper as I tried to shift them open.

I don't know what it was about her presence there, but I knew I couldn't do this without her. She was the one thing I needed desperately to hold on to in this world. My mom and my sister were now both gone. My club brother was gone too. There was just Kent, the little man, and me left now. The weight of that thought sunk me. It just completely ripped me apart inside. I would never get to see my sister again. Never get to watch Bender be so fuckin in love with her that it both disgusted and elated me to see it. The disgust had only come into play in the times I accidentally caught them up to no good at the clubhouse. She was still my little sister, and I never lost the urge to want to beat the shit out of him. At the same time, there was never anyone better for my sister. As the devastation of their loss settled into deep in my bones, I felt Poppy's arms wrap around me and pull me into her middle. She held me there while I came undone in her arms. Her warmth and strength wrapped around me like a favorite blanket. Comfort. That's what she was, comfort personified.

"Shh," she whispered as her kips touched brushed through the hair on my head. "I'm here. Chief's here. Whatever you need, we are here for you, Love, I promise."

The emptiness in my heart filled upon hearing her call me Love. It filled and helped pushed away the excruciating pain of loss. I knew it was only a momentary patch, but I was thankful for it. For her. For family that was still here. Kent was still here too. I needed to talk to him.

"I need to get ahold of Kent," I told her as I moved back in order to wipe my pathetic tears away from my face. It was only then that I realized Poppy hadn't come in alone.

"I already did, Brother." Chief came closer so he could speak softly since little man was still knocked out. "They were already in the air headed to Anaheim to play the Ducks. The team is sending him back the minute the land." That sounded familiar. I was pretty sure Ghost had told me something about California when I first got to the hospital, but it all slipped through the cracks considering everything that was being thrown at me.

"That's good then." I felt that familiar fog from yesterday try to swamp me and take me under again. I couldn't allow that. There was too much to do. Vengeance to be had, a little boy to care for, and a brother to get through the grieving process along me. Then there was the club, grieving for the brother they had lost and a fine old lady who had been as involved in the club as women could be. I wondered if Kent would be allowed any time off at all for everything that was headed our way with the preparations, funerals, and the world of hurt that would follow us through it all. "Do they know all of it yet?"

Chief shook his head in the negative. "Ghost has people working on it now. It won't take long."

"I need to get in touch with Shep and let him know, just in case." Worry coursed through me for his family. We had already connected the bombing and fires to the Russian Mafia. There was no stopping those types of people once they had their minds set on things.

"Ghost went to loop him in," Chief told me. I saw what looked like pride tipping the edges of Chief's lips up as he glanced over at Poppy. "She was telling me that Shep should be made aware just in case, and Ghost overheard. He assured us that Poppy was right, and he was headed over to do just that so we could be here for you and Brant."

I slid my hand down to Poppy's thigh and squeezed as she continued to hold me and rub little circle patterns into my back. I hadn't been wrong when I equated her to comfort earlier. She was the best kind of woman; one made to be an old lady and make sure her man was cared for and shit was handled when he couldn't be there to do it. Her soon-to-be ex-husband had to be off his fucking rocker not to see what he had in her. Still, I thanked the universe and beyond for his stupidity, because it led her right to me, and I wasn't fucking stupid. I squeezed again and then spoke softly to her. "I need to talk to Chief a minute. Could you sit with Brant?"

"Of course, but um, what if he wakes?"

"Just distract him as best you can until I get back. I won't be long." I managed to get up and out of the chair, despite my stiff back, before I leaned in and kissed the top of her head, smelling the sweet vanilla shit she used in her hair. Once I was up on my feet, I spun her around and helped her down into the chair that had been killer on my body as I attempted to sleep in it during the night. Then I took off with Chief in tow, making sure the door shut quietly behind us.

I turned to see Hopper in a chair outside of the door. "You mind sitting a bit longer? I need to go grab some food, and I don't want to leave the two of them."

"You don't even have to ask, brother. That's why I'm here. If it ain't me, another brother will be along to take a shift as long as your boy's here."

My boy. Jesus, fuck! It hit me right in the gut all over again, because with my sister and Bender gone, that's exactly what Brantley had just become. My boy. Not just my nephew, but mine to raise from now until he reached manhood. I wasn't scared to take it on. Hell, I'd already been down this road before after my mom got sick and then passed. My siblings became my kids to worry about in a weird way. Now, my nephew had stepped into that same role. Would the cycle ever end? I would never turn away family, but I was tired of losing pieces of it at the same time.

We didn't manage to even make it to the cafeteria before both of our phones pinged with incoming texts.

Poppy – Brant is awake. He asked why the big truck crunched them. He's asking for his momma, and I don't know what to tell him.

"I guess food will have to wait." I turned on my heel to go back the way we'd come and had taken a few steps before I realized Chief wasn't with me. He was still reading his message.

"I'll come up too, in case either of you needs me, and then head back down to grab food for everyone once we make sure Brant's okay. They'll probably both need a rescue by the time we get back."

"What's that mean?"

"It means that little boy is going to break my sister's heart wide open, and in response she'll smother the poor guy in goopy girly lovin'. I'm sure they'll both need a reprieve by the time you get there." He shrugged his shoulders. "Figured you could handle one, while I take the other out in the hallway and let her get it all out where he can't see."

It was the first thing that brought a smile to my face in two days. I could picture that happening. Though, if I knew my nephew at all, he would just eat up all the pretty girl lovin'.

"Thanks man," I called out as I jogged off in the direction of the room Brant was currently staying in with Chief following close at my heels.

When I got back to the room, a nurse was doing something off to the side and writing in a tablet. Poppy looked to me with desperation in her eyes. We hadn't been able to talk, and that was my fault. I should have filled her in on what I told Brantley before I left her alone with him.

"Hey, little man, you hangin' in there?"

"Unc Moke," he slurred a bit. "My gots owies."

"I know you have owies, Brant. The doctors are fixing you up as quick as they can so you can be even stronger when you leave here."

"Me Batman?" His sleepy question made me smile again for the second time today.

"Yeah, Bud, just like Batman." I could see he was having a hard time keeping his eyes open at that point, and I glanced over to the nurse, concerned since he'd just woken up. Why the hell would he still be sleepy. I didn't know if he had head trauma that was worse than just the bruising or what. Shit, the explanations we had gotten from the doctor seemed to blend together almost as if Charlie Brown's teacher had been giving his diagnosis. I knew it happened to people who were in shock, but I'd never experienced it before. When it was my mom going through stuff, she was the one to explain things to me, and she made sure I was really hearing all of it.

"I gave him a little something for the pain, but unfortunately it will make him super sleepy," the nurse finally told me after realizing I wasn't entirely sure what was happening. Her eyes softened as she glanced down at my nephew and patted his little head gently with her hand. "Probably for the best, considering." She turned her attention to Poppy again before speaking. "Just hit the button and call again if you need anything. I'm not sure if they'll be moving him upstairs to the pediatric wing or not. I do know they want to keep him here for at least 48 hours to watch and make sure there weren't any internal injuries that didn't present right away."

"Thank you," Poppy told her, and then the nurse took off out of the room like the hounds of hell were chasing after her. I caught Chief's grin and wondered if the bastard had been giving her 'fuck me' eyes the whole time or what. She had been cute. Not cute enough for me to really pay much attention to, but then again, no one could compare to the woman watching us with worried eyes.

"What exactly did he say?" I asked her now that we were alone in the room again.

She seemed to hesitate at first, and I wasn't sure why until she began telling me. Poppy probably wanted to spare me the details that my nephew had shared with her, but no matter how much they hurt we needed to know everything. "He told me his momma was screaming and then she wasn't. Then he asked why the big truck crunched them. He was in a lot of pain. That's really all he said other than to tell me he hurt."

I had to take a seat to absorb that information. We already knew that they'd been run off the road purposely, but to hear that my nephew knew it too, and that my sister had... Shit. I just couldn't think about it right now. I took a seat in the chair beside Brant's bed and pulled Poppy down on my lap needing to feel close to her. I needed something that could ground me and hold me together, because I had a little boy counting on me not to lose my shit.

We sat there quietly, just breathing each other in for a while. I didn't even notice when Chief left the room. Only that sometime later, it became apparent that we were alone. "Thank you for being here with him."

"You don't have to thank me for that. I know what it's like to lose almost your entire family. He's so young though."

"He is. I'm going to need you, and I don't think it's fair to ask this of you, considering."

She stopped me there. "You don't even have to ask, Love. I'm here for whatever you both need. I'm not going anywhere."

"Thank you," I whispered into her hair, feeling an immediate sense of relief. Things were still so new for us that I hated making demands on her time. Maybe I'd never have the words to convey what it meant to me, but I held her tighter and just breathed her in, hoping that somehow the feelings would convey through osmosis or some shit.

I'm not sure how long we sat we sat vigil at Brant's side, me in the hospital chair and Poppy in my lap, but a while later Shep, Ghost, and Leanne came bounding through the door. Ghost and Leanne seemed to be trying to hold Shep back, but he shrugged them off and looked completely devastated as he took in my little black and blue nephew lying there on the bed.

"No!" Shep choked out on a sob. "Tell me this isn't my doing." Fucking hell. I knew this would hit him hard since he got us involved in his family's business, but I wasn't sure I was ready for the reality of his reaction right now. Not here, in front of my nephew's hospital bed. I turned all my attention to him as he stood there, shoulders shaking and diving deep in that pit of despair and self-loathing. "I'm sorry. I'm so sorry." He kept mumbling.

"This isn't on you," I managed to get out in between his 'I'm sorry' litany. "This is not on you. This is on the fuckers who thought it was okay to run my sister and her family off the road. We will get them. They will die for this. All I need you to do is make sure your mom and sister are somewhere safe until we do. Send them away if you can. If you can't, let us know, and we'll see if one of the other chapters can house them for a while."

Shep's head shook back and forth almost violently. "No, look what happened when I got your guys involved before. I can't. I won't let you take on anything else."

"They killed my sister," I hissed back at him. "This is out of your hands now. Take care of your family so they don't end up dead too. We will get the bastards who did it."

"Jesus, I can't believe I did this."

"You did not do this!" I whisper-yelled, trying not to disturb Brantley while getting my point across. "No one in this damn room is responsible for this happening. You hear me? Any one of us would choose to help you out all over again if you called, even knowing what might happen. It's the life we live, man. We don't let family down, and you are my family too. So, let go of the guilt, and just worry about getting the women out of town."

"What about your woman?" Shep finally asked as he took in Poppy sitting there watching everything go down.

"We've got her, and all the rest handled. Everyone's on lockdown for now. They'll be plenty safe. Don't worry about us. Worry about your family, and if we need to get them out of town we will. The Dakotas will take them for sure, probably Sierra High too, maybe they can even stay with the girls of S.H.E. down there?" I turned my attention to Ghost, silently asking him if that was okay, or if I was stepping over a line.

"Already put in a call. Angel Girl said they'd take them in, no problem. They also volunteered some people if we need them. Keys and Quickshot are working their collective magic as we speak to get us the information we need to find these bastards."

"See, we have this covered," I offered up as reassurance.

Shep didn't say anything else for a long time, he simply stood there watching Brant as his chest rose and fell peacefully. "What's going to happen to little man now?"

"He's going to stay with me," I explained with no hesitation.

"Does he know?"

"Not yet." I told him. I'd talked to Brant about the fact that I wasn't going to leave him, but I didn't think he understood what that meant just yet. Hell, I wasn't so sure he'd even remember the conversation we had since I hadn't realized they'd been giving him some pretty strong medications for the pain. "How the hell is a someone so small supposed to comprehend that his family is gone?"

I must have spoken the question aloud because Poppy answered me. "He'll get through, because not all of his family is gone. He has you, Kent, and the club at his back. He won't want for anything."

"Except his parents," I muttered, hoping she was the only one who would hear that part.

"There's no helping that part, but we'll get him through it."

10. SAYING GOODBYE

ARRANGING THE FUNERAL OF MY LITTLE SISTER IS NOT SOMETHING I ever thought I would have to do in my lifetime. I always figured as the oldest sibling; I would be the one going out first. Arguing with my little brother over every detail was also something I didn't think I'd have to do. Kent had taken the bad news and immediately put it off on the club, as if we had all caused this shit to happen personally.

"They don't have any right to be involved!" His voice rose as we stood there looking at caskets that would hold our sister and her husband. Bender didn't have family outside of the club, so his arrangements fell on our shoulders too. Ghost had already tried to take that burden from me, but I wouldn't hear of it. Bender and Soph would want to go out together in every way. I was going to see to it that they did. I sighed at the thought before turning to my brother.

"Bender was a member of the club. Soph was heavily involved. The club was their family just as much as we are. They would both be extremely disappointed if the rest of their family were banned from coming to say their farewells, little brother."

"The club got them both killed and took them away from their son. I don't think they'd care about that right now."

"The club didn't get them killed."

"You're saying this wasn't the result of something the club did?"

"I'm saying the club got involved in the business of a private family with no affiliation, because they were in danger. We saved their lives. Bender would do it all over again if he were here to make that decision. No one knew what the fallout from helping other people would be, but you know what? I fuckin' do it every day. If not for the club, I do it for the department. You gonna shun the men from my firehouse if I die in a fire?"

I could see his anger burning underneath the surface, but I didn't stop there. "If you were to die on the ice in some freak accident, or because some punk-ass fucker from another team took a pot shot that went wrong, am I supposed to blame your whole team and tell them they can't show up to pay their respects?"

"It's not the same!" He yelled out, face red with the frustration I knew he was feeling. He wanted something tangible to blame, and the club fit the bill, even if he knew deep down that they weren't really responsible.

"It's exactly the same, and as soon as you pull your head out of your ass and realize that you're going to feel like a jackass for shitting on your sister's family when they're all devastated at her death just as we are."

"You're comparing them to our blood bond?"

"No, I'm fucking not. The difference is, we are blood bonded. They chose to be in her life, and they want to be there to celebrate it and say goodbye. It's not a choice for us because we are blood. They took her in and loved her just because they wanted to. That's the difference. The only difference, Kent. My club will be the ones taking care of Brantley when I'm on shift, or if something comes up. They are the family that Brant knows more so than you since your schedule keeps you away so often. They will be there for him. If for no fucking other reason, they will be there because that little boy can't take losing any more family right now and those men are his uncles. The women are his aunts. He needs them. He expects them to be there, and saying goodbye is something that is more important for him than any of the rest of us so we're going to honor that, whether you like it or not."

"Fuck you, man!" Kent shouted before storming away. I knew he'd put it all together and get with the program. He just needed time to grieve and work through the anger over losing our sister so pointlessly.

The funeral director approached me wearily for my choice of caskets. "We'll take two. One in black and the other white," I told him. Black for Granger and the white for Sophie."

"Yes sir, I will make sure everything is set. We have all of your other choices?"

"You do," I told him. Even though every other choice we had made was like pulling teeth from Kent, we managed to agree on all of the little stuff aside from the guest list. There was no way I was keeping the club away from their funeral though. It didn't matter how big a fit Kent threw. If he even thought to cause a scene at the funeral, I would toss him in the goddamn hole waiting to hold my sister and club brother. Someone else could fish his cantankerous ass out of it.

My phone pinged and when I glanced down, it was a text from Quickshot.

Quickshot: Think we found something.
Tracking real estate. There's a couple places
not too far away.

Smoke: Send the addresses, and we'll run
them down.

Quickshot: I'll send them after the funeral.

Smoke: Send now, or there will be another
funeral you won't have a choice in
attending.

Quickshot: Damn it, Smoke. You have too
much going on right now.

Smoke: Right. So don't fuck with me.

Quickshot: Sent.

Smoke: Did not receive.

Quickshot: Sent to Ghost. You can get the
info from him.

That fucker. I'd always respected the man especially

since he went to go help start one of our new chapters about a decade ago. You had to respect a man who would move away from everything he knows in order to get out from under the shadow of his father and the other men who had raised him. On second thought, maybe he took the easy way out by doing it. Who knew? The only thing I knew in that moment was that when I saw Quickshot again, he had an ass whooping coming to him.

I wondered briefly if I had been able to go with them to Georgia back then, would I have met Poppy sooner? I let the fleeting thought go just as quickly as it had come. While I'd felt abandoned by the younger generation of Aces High Cedar Falls at the time, there was no way I could have up and moved states away when I was taking care of my siblings. They had already been through enough.

Still, back then, there was something calling me to join them, if only my circumstances had been different. Maybe we weren't ready for one another then. The way Chief talks about how in love his sister and Walker were in the beginning, I probably wouldn't have stood a chance. Then I would have been just another Snake pining over another man's woman. Yeah, I knew about him. I also knew that Poppy never gave a single thought as to what it would be like to jump from her man to him. Part of that was probably because she knew Snake was well aware of the shady business her ex had been getting up to and he stuck by the code and never told her.

I shook off all my wandering thoughts when I realized I was standing in the fucking funeral home looking at caskets. Moments like these made me question if I was losing my goddamn mind. My fingers slid along the showroom casket I had chosen for my sister and brother-in-law. They would be buried side-by-side, just the way they had lived their lives since meeting one another. It was a fitting tribute, the last I could give them besides making sure their son was taken care of and raised up to be the man they'd both be proud of. Another incoming text pulled me out of the morose thoughts that were starting to swarm.

Chief: Is little man with Poppy?

Smoke: yeah

Chief: Kent is asking to see him.

Smoke: Supervised only. He doesn't have to know that. Kent's not taking shit well, and he's blaming the club.

Chief : I figured that when he demanded I bring his nephew to him away from the shit hole den of evil.

Smoke: Fuck me. He walks his ass into the den and deals with the devil in order to see his nephew. Not gonna have him saying vile shit to the kid. Club is his family. This ain't the time.

Chief: Agreed. I'll supervise if it comes to it.

Chief: He'll come around. He just needs someone to blame right now.

Smoke: I know it. Doesn't mean I like it.

Chief: I'll keep you updated.

Smoke: Where's Ghost?

Chief: took off with Tuck and Hopper to go run something down.

Smoke: Fuck.

Chief: Go get a shower and some clean clothes on. You're starting to smell

Smoke: You can't smell through texts, asshole.

Chief: That's how bad you are.

I didn't bother responding, and instead, glanced down at myself. I was still wearing the same fucking clothes I'd been in days ago when I was told to haul ass home for yet another emergency. Chief might have had a valid point. When I managed to get back to my apartment and hop off my bike, I could have sworn I saw a familiar car sitting there in the lot. It couldn't be though. She wouldn't have the stones to come around me during a time like this. Would she? I shook it off and went inside. No way was that my ex, Julie, sitting out there.

I don't know that getting a shower and putting clean clothes on made me feel any better, but it certainly rejuvenated me a bit. I grabbed a quick bite to eat as well before texting Ghost.

> Smoke: Whatever Quickshot sent to you, I need to know.

Ghost: 2233 Forest Side Ave.

That was all he sent. I tossed the address into the GPS on my phone, connected the Bluetooth in my helmet, and headed that way. The open road is a funny thing. We all talk about the freedom we feel when we ride, but part of that freedom is in being able to just let it all go. The negative thoughts, the shit that bogs you down, all of it just flows off with the wind in your face and the feeling of flying. Not to say it doesn't come rushing back the minute the engine is cut, but for those moments when the road has your focus, you become one with the journey, no matter how lengthy or short. The rest of the shit in your life just falls away until you reach your destination.

In this case, my destination was an older, two story brick home. It was unassuming, a little off to itself, but not unlike the other houses that I'd passed to get here. The faded blue shutters looked like they'd seen better days and the lawn was slightly overgrown as if the house had been vacant, or simply uncared for by its owners. There were three other bikes pulled all the way up into the driveway, so I assumed the house had been sitting vacant for a good while.

Ghost stepped out the front door and waved me on up as I parked my bike facing out toward the street. I didn't even make it into the house before the smell hit me. "What the fuck?"

"Looks like someone was tipped off that they might be getting a visit here. They left their supply behind," he offered up grimly. Supply? What the fuck kind of supply smelled like rotting corpses?

I got my answer once I managed to move past the smell and down into the basement level of the house. There, cages lined the walls. There were four down one side and they didn't go to the ceiling. They were about four feet tall from ground to top and looked more like something you would set up if you were kenneling dogs. The bodies inside some of the cages were not dogs, though it didn't appear they were treated much better. There were literally dog dishes set inside the cages that had once held food and water, or at least that's what I hoped they had been placed there for. Fecal matter and piss stained the far corners of the cages and small, thin bedding was placed to one side. The bedding was no more than tattered blankets on the floor. The women – because that's what they had once been – inside each cage were pitiful looking remnants of what they once had been.

There wasn't much left to the four of them, each in a cage of their own. Three were in cages on the left side of the room while the fourth was off to herself in a cage on the right. It wasn't clear how long they'd been dead, but judging by the smell, I'd say at least a few days. A small choked cough coming from the far right cage where the lone girl was kept startled all of us, and Hopper quickly jumped to action.

"Fucking hell, I thought they were all gone!" Ghost yelled from behind my shoulder.

"We all thought that, judging by the smell and the shape they're in," Hopper answered back as he used bolt cutters to pop the lock on the cage.

"Check the others," Ghost ordered. Tuck and I immediately moved to open the other cages, but the three women on that side of the room were long gone. I came out after checking the last of them to find Hopper carrying the ghost of a woman up the stairs.

"Jesus, I can't believe she's alive. Did you see her?" Tuck asked.

"She might not be for much longer. Hop's taking her to Doc Burns."

"Let's hope she can last long enough to help us catch these pricks," I muttered.

Ghost shook his head. "I wouldn't hold your breath on that," he insisted, and while I knew he wasn't wrong, I still hoped.

"That could have been Sophie," I managed to choke out. "If she hadn't died, they could have taken her, and this could have been her life."

The look on Ghost's face nearly buckled my knees as my words sunk in. He pulled his cell out and dialed someone. "No women and children allowed out of the compound for any reason without an escort until further notice. Keep a heavy guard on them." He listened for a moment and then tucked his phone back in his pocket. It was a good call. These assholes had already proven they didn't mind taking women and children out. The last thing we needed was for an old lady or any of the kids to go missing and end up in a place like this, left to die after suffering unimaginable shit.

"We need to find these bastards and take them the fuck out." My words were a demand. Ghost only nodded his head. Obviously, he felt the same way. "I'm putting in a call to Jamie. They dealt with traffickers in their territory before. Hopefully, their experience will be helpful."

"Are they coming in for the..." I couldn't bring myself to say the fucking word. It was like the word funeral was stuck in my throat and refused to come out. Maybe if I didn't say it, I wouldn't have to live through watching my little sister be lowered into the cold, unforgiving ground.

"They are. I'm going to make some calls and get someone busy cleaning up this fucking tragedy." He turned his watchful gaze on me. "You should get back to the clubhouse and check on Poppy and Brant."

Brantley had been released from the hospital the day before. I'd stayed with him at the clubhouse that night but left him with Poppy and the women of the club afterward. I had too much on my mind, and too many things to do today, like picking out caskets and tracking down the leftovers and trash of a group of men who never saw those women for what they really were. People, who deserved to be treated better than lab rats locked in cages, only to be used until there was nothing left.

"Do you think she'll want to live after what she went through?" I asked, thinking of the woman who had been taken away by Hopper.

Ghost shook his head. "She'll have to be pretty strong to come back from this physically, brother. Not sure there's a strong enough mentality to wash this kind of shit from a person's soul though."

That's what I had been thinking too. "Might want to make sure she gets put on a suicide watch if she pulls through. We're going to need her to talk."

He scrubbed a hand down his stubbled jaw, turquoise eyes moving off to stare at the cinder block wall coated in grime. "Much as it pains me to feel like we're using her just as much, I know it's necessary."

I nodded and moved to get up the stairs. "Heading out. Still have some arrangements to make."

"You don't have to do all this shit alone, Smoke."

"I know it, but I need to."

11. A TOMB

WALKING INTO MY SISTER'S HOUSE WAS LIKE MOVING THROUGH A tomb. Everything was quiet and undisturbed. There were things thrown about haphazardly, no doubt from when they'd gotten ready to go on their little family trip. It looked like they walked out the door expecting to come and pick back up where they left off in their life. Soph and Bender would never get that chance again though. They'd reached their ends, and now I had to go through their shit to find outfits to bury them in. It wasn't fucking right. We couldn't even have an open casket for either of them because of the trauma they'd both suffered to their faces. Still, I wasn't going to disrespect them by sending either of them off to another life in anything less than the best. Didn't matter who saw. Maybe the thing you wore when you died was what you spent your eternity wearing. Maybe, you got to choose to slip into your funeral best? Who the fuck knew? I sure as fuck didn't.

I climbed the stairs to the master suite and glanced around at the unmade bed, the few pieces of clothing strewn about still. My sister had trouble deciding what to wear again and never bothered to clean up before they left. It was typical of her, and seeing that remnant of her personality was like drilling a spike right through my damn heart. Jesus. I took a breath, and another before I found myself sitting on the edge of her bed crying for their loss all over again. "I'm so fucking sorry, Sis."

I gave myself a few minutes to give in to the grief I was feeling and to mourn two of the most beloved people in my life. Then I hauled myself up off of their bed and moved to the closet where his clothes hung on the left side and hers were on the right. It smelled like a mixture of the two of them in there and knocked me back once more. I could close my eyes, inhale, and it was as if they were standing there with me.

"You can do this," I could hear my sister telling me in her sweet, encouraging voice.

"Take care of my boy," Bender's voice seemed real as the deep baritone resonated through me. I'd swear they were really there talking to me, even though I knew it was all in my own head.

"I will not let you down," I promised them both as I grabbed some clothes I thought they'd want to wear to their own send-off and got the hell out of there before I decided to never leave the comfort of their imagined embrace.

My next stop was Brantley's room across the hall. I took an old diaper bag out of the closet and started filling it with some of his clothes, a few of his favorite toys, and bath time stuff before I called it good.

TWO DAYS LATER, I was on my way to the graveside service for both Bender and my sister when I remembered our mother's necklace. I turned around and headed in the other direction to Sophie's house in order to retrieve it, because I wanted it to go with Sophie so she and mom could be together in death in some way. It was probably stupid, but I couldn't get it out of my mind, so I followed my gut. I was about to call Poppy and tell her I'd be running a little late and ask her to meet me there, but my cell was dead. I knew it wasn't fair, me leaving Brantley with her all this time while I was out trying to run down leads, but I couldn't stop or I'd think and fall apart. All I had to keep me sane was diving headfirst into anything that kept me too busy to think about what today meant for my family.

It took me far too long to find where Sophie had the damn necklace hiding. Once I found it and looked at the clock on her wall, I realized I might be cutting it close just getting to the cemetery on time. I'd never hear the end of it from Kent if that happened so I tried to haul my ass there quickly.

As if someone out there in the cosmos was trying to fuck with me, I heard my name called the minute I parked my bike. I ignored it and started walking at a brisk pace toward the area where I could see everyone gathered. I was nearly there, just on the outskirts of the mourners who had gathered when a manicured set of nails wound around my upper arm and pulled tightly, forcing me to stop where I was by a tree.

"What the fuck?"

"Oh God! Smoke, I'm so sorry about Soph." It hit me then, the sickeningly sweet smell of her perfume.

"Julie?" I questioned just as she managed to latch onto me like a suckerfish. It was an apt description too, because I had zero doubts that she was going to try to use my sister's death and my grief as a way to get her foot back in the door with me. She was dead fucking wrong about that. I reached up and attempted to pry her off of me, but I had my mother's necklace clasped tightly in the one hand, and didn't want to drop it so my efforts were hampered a bit. The more I tried to get her off of me the harder she would cling. I was nearing the point of losing my fucking mind with her when I heard Brantley call out to me.

"Unc Moke!" My attention snapped directly to him, and the person carrying him, in time to see the weary look on her face. Shit. Just fucking great. I couldn't even come to grieve my family's deaths and say goodbye without Julie causing a scene and fucking shit up with the woman I had been neglecting. It would be my luck Poppy would think Julie had been where I was spending all of my time away from her and Brant. It didn't help matters that everyone else was now watching too as Chief walked over to Poppy and whispered something to her before tossing a glare back at me over his shoulder.

"Let the fuck go, now!" I demanded of Julie. I don't know

if she heard the threat in my voice or not, but she let go and looked up at me with wide, innocent eyes.

"Smoke, I just want to be here for you."

"Yeah? If that were the case, you wouldn't have just caused a fuckin' scene at my sister's funeral. Now, get the fuck off of me!" I told her again. She had eased off of her hold before, but her fingers still clung to the front of my kutte as if she were holding on to a lifeline. She no longer had access to that shit, and I wasn't playing games with her thinking that she could just waltz back into my life.

"Poppy!" I called as I started moving towards where she was headed. I was confused at first, because it looked like she was trying to leave the funeral with Brant. That wasn't fucking right. He should be here to say goodbye to his mom and dad.

She managed to get all the way to her car before I caught up and grabbed hold of her elbow to keep her from getting herself or Brant inside.

"You might want to back off a minute, Brother," Chief demanded.

"Seriously?" I asked, taken aback by the order coming from my club brother.

"Seriously," Chief answered as he maneuvered me back a bit so Poppy could get my nephew strapped into his car seat in her car.

"What's going on?"

Chief stood back as Poppy finished and then turned to me looking ready for a fight. "I'm taking Brant home, because he's tired, and I think he's had enough today. I've been answering questions all day for him about why we were saying goodbye to the boxes when his mom and dad are in heaven. Why can't we go to heaven to see them? Why can't they come visit? Why didn't they take him with them? It's been nonstop. Frankly, I'm not even sure I'm telling him the right things, but you haven't been around to ask. Kent is angry with me for some reason and won't speak to me. You've been God knows where with Lord only knows who, and I just can't help thinking I'm the last person your sister would have wanted answering these questions for her son. She only met me the one time, and she didn't have a high opinion of me for at least half of that time." She blew out a sharp breath once she was through speaking and stood there staring back and forth between myself and Chief.

"You look tired," Chief's soft words for his sister made me take notice of the dark circles under her eyes. "I'll come back with you and watch Brant so you can get a nap, okay?"

"There's no need for that. I was planning on heading out with them when they went," I responded to Chief before she could.

"Really? Up until they spotted you with your ex hanging all over you, Poppy wasn't even aware you had shown up for the funeral. She didn't know if she'd see you there at all before she left. I get that you have a lot going on right now, man, but that kid ain't hers. It isn't her responsibility to do all the tough stuff with him, and have you come in once the dust has settled and finally decide that you have time for him. My sister isn't your damn nanny, and you need to remember that. She's already had one man treat her like she was only good for keeping his house when he wanted to be there. She doesn't need a repeat performance with extra responsibilities thrown in for fun."

"Jesus, Chief!" I ground out, raising my voice a little more than I wanted to. "You know where I've been! I've been hunting down the maniacs who took my fucking sister. You'd be doing the same goddamn thing!" I took a step back, trying to shake off the anger I was feeling in the moment before I continued on. "Look, I don't know how to do this. He's my nephew, and I've watched him before, but I've never had to prioritize him before like this. I don't know what to do here, because I can't let Soph and Bender's deaths go unanswered. I can't exactly take Brant with me when I do those things. I'll find someone else who can help with him for the time being if it's a problem. I didn't mean to put the burden on Poppy." I turned to her, to make sure she knew I meant what I was saying. "I didn't mean to leave you holding my family's bag, I swear."

"Brant is not a burden. Not knowing what you expect me to say to him or do with him is though. I can't be the one making the decision about what to tell him about his parents, or how to cope, or God, any of it. I can't because I didn't know how to do those things for myself when I lost my family and I was an adult."

"Plus, she hasn't been feeling well. Not that she'd tell anyone and admit she's not perfect," Chief informed me, and I felt my stomach drop.

"What?" Poppy huffed out in a shrill tone as she stared daggers at her brother.

"Saw you get sick this morning," he told her while

looking her over as if he could see inside of her and all of her secrets were suddenly clear to him.

"Probably just something I ate," she managed to spit back out at him.

"You were sick?" I tried to clarify as I took in her less than stellar pallor and again, those darkened circles. I had thought she was just tired, but I supposed they'd be there if she was sick too.

"Yeah, something you may have noticed if you'd even checked in with her for more than two minutes a day," Chief stated, not leaving out the disdain he felt as it dripped from his words to my ears.

"Shit," I huffed. "How about we get you guys home, and then we'll figure everything out where you can relax?" Poppy didn't answer, instead I watched as her attention shifted beyond where we were all standing by her car to someone not too far off. It took a moment for me to track her field of vision and then put two and two together with what she was seeing. "No," I told her as I pointed to her car. "Get in, drive home, and I'll meet you there." We were not going to focus on Julie, or the fact that she'd been standing there watching us. She wasn't even on my radar before and I wouldn't waste a moment more thinking of her. All I wanted was to get Poppy and Brant home and just be at peace with them.

On my way to my bike to follow them, I texted her to meet me at her own house. I wanted to stay there with my woman and my nephew away from the prying eyes of the club for a little bit. I needed some normalcy without the pity-laced looks being thrown at me, or worse, the concerned looks from those who were wondering when I was going to flip my shit and forget the need to be discrete while seeking my vengeance.

When I got to the house and she didn't answer the door right away, I moved to go through the gate on the side of the house in order to get into the backyard. "Figured you were out here when you didn't answer."

"What if I just wasn't up for company and ignoring you?"

I could tell by her response that she had been dwelling on the scene she'd witnessed with Julie's suckerfish imperson-ation, so I didn't bother to wait to clarify that. "I haven't seen or spoken to Julie in six months until this morning. She heard about Soph and showed up, caught up to me as I heading to the," once again I found that the word just wouldn't leave my throat. It was stuck there again. "What you saw wasn't-"

Poppy threw her hands up in the air to wave away what I'd been about to say. "Stop. It doesn't matter, because the only reason I entertained doubts was because of your behavior over the past few days. Had you been around at all, helping with Brantley, I would have never thought..."

Shit!

My whole body slumped in on itself with her words. She was right. I had done this. By not being present in their lives, I had given her reason to doubt.

"I couldn't stop. I couldn't sit still. In the brief minutes when I do, everything is real and she's never coming back. She was my little sister, but I raised her too. After my dad left, when my mom had to work so much, it was me looking after them. They're like my kids in a way, and now," I swal-lowed down the emotion that was clogging my ability to speak. "She's gone and Kent won't speak to me, because he thinks it's my fault. I don't know what to do with all that."

"I understand. I really, honestly do understand what you're going through. That doesn't make it easier when I have a past that clouds everything in muck. I know that shouldn't fall on you, but I can't help the way I feel or that I'm questioning everything now, because I didn't question enough before."

I stepped closer to her and reached out to pull her to me. "I'm sorry, Poppy." I clung to her, inhaling her familiar scent, taking comfort in her presence, and then I felt it all over again. That desperate ache where my vibrant sister used to fill the space with happiness. The spot in my heart where Bender used to tell his ridiculous jokes and make me laugh. Those spots I didn't think would ever feel full again threatened to drown me as my body shook with the effort to hold off the grief a little longer. Inhale – the subtle, sweet vanilla scent that lingered around Poppy. Exhale – all the memories that were threatening to pull me under. It took a few minutes before I was able to pull it together, and she must have sensed the shift, because she waited until that moment to speak.

"Will they come for us too?"

"No!" I answered on instinct. "I've had Gray watching out for you two."

"Surfer-dude?"

I grinned at her. "Yeah, surfer-dude. He's been watching the house when I haven't been here."

"I haven't seen a bike out there the past few days."

"That's because he's been incognito in a fucking cage.

Listen, Poppy, I know what you were thinking and I just need you to understand that you weren't forgotten. You haven't been far from my mind, in fact, I've been gone so much to make sure you don't end up like Soph. I want you and Brant safe even if that means I can't be here while I'm hunting for the assholes who destroyed my family."

12. TORN

POPPY SEEMED FAR MORE EXHAUSTED THAN I HAD GIVEN HER CREDIT for at the cemetery. By the time we got home she could barely keep her eyes open and I did my best to convince her just to go take a nap. I thought she would just go down for a quick nap, but when I called her for dinner and she didn't even stir, I figured she needed the break more than I thought so I let her be.

"Is Popwee otay?" Brant asked while we were eating some pizza for dinner.

"She's okay, little man, just tired."

"Popwee is sick. She frowned up."

"I know. Chief told me."

"Teef is Popwee's brudder like you mommy's brudder?"

"Yeah," I managed to get out before I had to turn away and pull myself together. "Chief is Poppy's brother."

"I miss my mommy," Brant spoke softly into the last of his pizza slice. I scooted him over from his booster seat onto my lap and we sat like that for a bit.

"I miss her too, little man. Every day," I stated solemnly, staving off another wave of overwhelming sadness. "What do you say we get you a bubble bath set up? I brought some of your toys from the house. You can pick two to take in the tub with you."

"Otay," he mumbled as his head continued to lie there on my chest. I knew then that missing his parents was getting to him more than he realized. The kid normally loved bubble baths more than any woman I'd ever met.

"Do you want to just sit here with me for a little while instead?"

His little hands fisted in the cotton of my t-shirt and pulled tight while I felt the tell-tale wetness from his tears. I ran my hand up and down his back and let him have his moment. I sat there rocking his little body against me for the longest time before I realized the wetness I was feeling on my shirt was no longer tears, but little boy drool. I carried him to the second bedroom that Poppy had managed to transform into a little boy's spot without me noticing over the past couple of days. I don't know how she managed to find the time, and I had a sneaking suspicion some of the old ladies must have helped out. It squeezed at my heart just a little bit more. I'd practically dumped my nephew in her lap, and she didn't complain about it. Instead, she made a home for him to fall into so he wouldn't feel so out of place.

Once I tucked his little body into bed, I turned and made sure the nightlight was on and watched as Bubba curled up beside the bed with his back to the bed and face toward the door. "Good boy, Bubba. You watch over my boy." Bubba snuffled as if to say, "Duh," to me and rested his snout on his paws. I moved through the house locking up, cleaning our mess, and then made my way to the other bedroom. Poppy was still knocked out and I didn't want to disturb her after all the shit I'd put off on her over the past week. Instead, I undressed down to my boxer briefs, crawled in beside her, and pulled her tight to my body.

Her sweet scent and warmth lulled me to sleep quickly, and it was the first peaceful night I'd spent since I left her in Pittsburgh with my brother. The fucking night where everything fell apart. I knew I would be distracted even more over the coming days as we started to get more intel on the bastards behind the barn explosions and my sister's death. It made me hold on tighter to the woman in my arms, because the bad shit wasn't behind us yet – not by a long shot.

I heard both Brant and Bubba stirring, and Poppy was still dead to the world, so I got up to go check on them and let Bubba out into the backyard. Once he did his business, I set about making Brant breakfast since I hadn't been around to do the little things with him since his release from the hospital. His bruised face was already starting to change colors with some shades of ugly yellow, green, and the deeper purples still lurking near the center of his wounds. He'd been lucky that he was still so small.

Glancing around Poppy's kitchen, it quickly became obvious that I would either have to go to the store or make do with what she had there. Eggs and pancakes it was. She did at least have a little orange juice I could give little man as well. I set about making breakfast and sneaking Brant a few football shaped pancakes before I heard Poppy up and moving in the other room.

"Poppy?" I called out, but she didn't answer right away and I assumed she was using the bathroom. I quickly lost my train of thought where she was concerned though when I saw one of the pancake footballs fly through the air and land in Bubba's mouth. Brant clapped furiously as the dog managed to catch the wobbly throw.

"Little man, those are not the kinds of balls we throw. You eat them, the dog doesn't."

"But he catched it."

"I saw that. Bubba's good at catching, but we don't throw food."

He huffed and stuffed another pancake football in his mouth before I heard the bathroom door open again. I didn't bother calling out to her this time and just waited for her to come and join us.

"Hey!" Her sleep roughened voice was sexy as fuck, but she wasn't looking to great, despite the nearly 16 hours of sleep she managed to pack in.

"Hey babe, we were just making pancakes for breakfast. Want some?"

"Sure."

"You were out of pretty much every breakfast meat," I explained to her as I held up the pan with the scrambled eggs in it. "I made eggs too though."

"I see that, thank you." She turned away from me quickly and tried to find something else to talk about for some reason. I figured she was still pissed at me for dropping my responsibilities in her lap, or maybe for the fact that my ex had latched on to me at the funeral yesterday and caused such a scene that I hadn't even been able to do what made me late in the first place. The necklace that had belonged to my mother was still in my pocket where I'd tucked it when I followed Poppy and Brant home yesterday.

Unfortunately, I didn't get to sit down and eat with her because about the time she started talking to Brant, my cell started ringing. I glanced over at Poppy feeling guilty as fuck, but knowing I needed to answer all the same. She gave me a wry smile and turned back to my nephew and humored him while I answered.

"Yeah," I called out to the phone. At first, I didn't tune in to whoever was speaking because all I could hear was Poppy and Brantley talking.

"Those are some pretty fancy looking pancakes you have, buddy," Poppy said to Brant as she leaned in and placed a sweet kiss on his head.

"Unc Moke told me no frowing dez balls."

Her laughter was a balm to my soul even if it wasn't directed toward me. "He's right. That would make a mess, and Bubba might eat them."

"Bubbsba wikes cancakes, Popwee."

"Yo! Smoke! I heard called out through the line. "Are you listening or what?"

"Sorry, my mind's elsewhere right now. What's going on?"

"We have something you might want to check out. Doc managed to get some information out of the girl, and Quick-shot and his woman ran with it. They think they have something."

If they had something, I had no choice but to go and handle business. I knew it wouldn't make Poppy happy. We needed to have a talk and I needed to not leave her with the kid I'd inherited. I felt bad and torn in so many different directions it physically hurt. I tuned back into my nephew and Poppy's conversation because he turned toward me with an accusing look.

"Because it's not good for him," Poppy was explaining as Brantley's mouth dropped open, and all I saw him pushing the pancakes out of his mouth with his tongue while he glared in my direction. Great, my nephew thought I was trying to poison him now.

"Cancakes bad?"

"Pancakes aren't bad for little boys, just doggies," she tried to explain.

"Why?"

"I don't know why. They just are."

My nephew eyeballed the dog for a minute before turning back to Poppy and telling her how it really was. "He wikes dem."

"Are you still there? We're meeting up in 15 at the club-house. Church for everyone in the know," Hopper informed me.

"I'll be there," I said as the line disconnected, and I stuffed the cell back in my pocket. "Hey babe," I called out to Poppy and watched as her shoulders stiffened. She knew what was coming, and her reaction made me feel even worse.

"You have to go?"

"Yeah, I do. I want to talk with you, but it's going to have to wait awhile. Are you okay with that?"

She sighed deeply, and I couldn't beat the feeling back

that I might be doing irreparable harm to our relationship. "Yeah, go do what you have to do."

"Pop, I don't want to go. This is important though."

"I get it, Smoke, really. Go; take care of your crap. We'll be fine."

"I'll send someone in a bit to grab Brant for a bit if I'm going to be too long. You need to be able to get your stuff done too, and I know that's not easy with a little one running around."

"It's fine. I'll let you know if I ever need help."

"I'll call you later and see how things are going." I set a plate loaded down with pancakes and eggs in front of her before I leaned in and kissed the top of her head and then reached over and did the same to Brant. "I'll be back later, lil man, you listen to Poppy, and be a good boy for me okay?"

"Otay, Unc Moke. Bye" He waved his syrup-laden fingers at me, and I just barely managed to dodge out of his reach before he swiped them down my kutte.

"Looks like you were right," Ghost told me as I sat down in my seat next to our road captain, Wren.

"Do I even want to know what I was right about?"

"The tattoos on the man you guys caught with Shep's family and the one on the thumb webbing of the digit you found at the barn fire are both Russian in nature. The second being the same thing that Gregor had on him when he used to hang around."

I nodded my head. "Have we found links between the dead guy and any specific group?"

"We did, but it's just a theory at this point. I have Quick-shot checking into shit still, but we're thinking the Stasevich Bratva is behind all of it."

"Never heard of them." There were a slew of Russian mafia type groups as well as Irish, Italian, and just mutt crews of punks who took street gangs one step further.

Ghost sighed deeply. "They're very much known for traf-ficking women, and sometimes children. It's all a matter of what brings in the most money for them."

"That's not really a surprise since they were willing to take Tammy and Lindsay as payment for Chad's debt," I told him.

"Don't think they gave two shits about Tammy. Lindsay, on the other hand, was worth quite a bit to them. From what Quick has been able to dig up so far, they wanted her because virgins sell at a premium, and Chad assured them she's a virgin."

"Fucking hell," I hissed. "Are we able to pass any of this along to Shep? He needs to know that they won't stop looking for her." I pounded my fist into the table in front of me. "Better yet, has Quick managed to get an address? Any kind of fuckin' location where we can get ahold of these bastards and end them?"

"He's still working on it, Smoke. You'll know as soon he does, I promise you that." He glanced around the table. "As for Shep and his family, you need to check in with him and see what he wants to do. You know we'd be glad to have him on board here with us, and if he makes that happen, it frees up a few places where our hands are tied. Family first. See if he's willing to put in the time to prospect."

"He rides a rocket not a cruiser," I mentioned and heard a few people snickering around the table.

Ghost shrugged his shoulders. "I know some clubs give a shit about that, but I don't. Riding is riding. He wants to be free in the wind on a fucking rice burner, then he can be."

"I'll check in with him and see what he wants to do." I stood to leave before turning back. "If he declines, will that affect his family being able to stay with the women in S.H.E.?"

"You know Angel Girl isn't going to turn them out," Ghost informed me. I didn't think she would, especially not the girl. Tammy was a different story though since she could be a bit difficult. "I'll keep you updated on their situation too so you can get word back to Shep." We had Shep locked down from talking to his family for all of their safety. I tipped my chin at Ghost, but before I managed to get out the door, he was speaking again. "You have work?"

"Nah, gotta take a leak," I explained why I had been so eager to get out the fucking door.

Ghost laughed. "Go take care of business, and then get back here. I'm going to put Angel Girl on and let you work shit out with how long the women will be down there, and what you think may need to happen with them from here on out."

"Sounds great." It did, until I got a text from Chief.

Chief: Might want to get to Poppy's ASAP.

Smoke: WTF?

Chief: Julie is here. Heading in now.

I ran back out to the large office area where we held church and ducked my head in. "Need to head to Poppy's really quick. Julie's there causing trouble. Be back when I get that shit sorted."

"Go!" Was all Ghost said, and I was on my fucking way to deal with the cunt that would not stop infecting my life with her bullshit.

SEEING Julie standing there just shy of the front stoop of Poppy's home pissed me off something fierce. I roared into the driveway, parking just to the rear and off to the right of Chief's bike so that I wouldn't be blocking him in. It was habit, because it sure as fuck wasn't what was on my mind. "What in the hell are you doing at this house?"

"Hey baby, I came by to pick up Brant. We talked about me taking care of him yesterday, remember."

"What the fuck kinds of drugs are you on? I told you my woman would be the one caring for Brant when you asked."

I watched as her head moved back and forth in a negative way as she smiled at me, eyes glazed over in a way I almost never saw from her when we were together. If I didn't know better, I'd say it looked like she was in love with me, but that was ridiculous because I'd left her in Pittsburgh without any hesitation after finding out about her betrayal, and what it had been costing me with my brother.

"Why are you here?" I snarled the words at her this time and watched as the hazy lovelorn look in her eyes finally started to clear.

"You told me I would be taking care of him."

"I fuckin' said my woman would be taking care of him." I threw my hand out, my forefinger pointing directly at my woman. "Poppy being that woman." I moved my hand back and forth between us, indicating who exactly I meant. "You and I haven't been together in six months. Why in the hell would you be the one caring for him?"

"You and Poppy?" She almost whispered in disbelief as she glanced between me and the woman she was just starting to understand meant something to me. "You're with her?"

"Yeah, like I told you yesterday." The fact that I was even having this conversation wasn't sitting well with me. Julie should have never been there at my sister's funeral to begin with. She knew she wasn't welcome around my siblings since she fucked with my relationship with Kent for years. I couldn't fathom how she walked away from our conversation there thinking that I had somehow changed my mind.

"I thought you just meant you had brought her with you to the cemetery, because she was caring for Brant temporarily. How is it possible you moved on so quickly?" Her voice took on that thick tone as if she were about to cry, but I couldn't find it in me to care that she was hurting, because right now she was starting shit with the woman I planned to spend the rest of my life with. If she ruined this for me with her antics, I wouldn't hesitate to put her in the fuckin' ground, and that wasn't something I took lightly.

"Julie, I told you when it was over that I meant it. Hell, you knew I'd been with other women since." I wasn't stupid. We had a former club whore, turned old lady, who still hung around on occasion and she had remained friends with Julie. I was sure she was passing information back to her whenever she saw me with anyone over the past six months.

"I thought Jewel was just telling me those things to make me jealous. I thought you just needed to get some things out of your system, because you were mad at me. You were supposed to come back to me. She said she'd help make sure you came back," Julie cried out, and I didn't miss the desperation in her voice. "Yesterday, I thought you were talking about-"

"How the hell did you know where to find Brant?" Chief was apparently just as tired of this shit as I was, and decided to move things along for us by asking one of the questions I had neglected to get at.

"I followed you here yesterday. At first, I thought you got a new house, but then I saw the car she got into yesterday too, and figured it was your babysitter's house." She spoke to me as if Chief hadn't asked, and I had. I didn't know if this part of her delusion, or if she just couldn't take her focus off of me. Either way, it had moved beyond creepy as fuck.

"Not my babysitter. She's my woman. You hear me? You are nothing to me. We are history, and it's a lesson I don't miss. You need to get that through your head and move the hell on. I catch you near Poppy, Brantley, my work, home, the club, or anywhere else, I will be forced to take action. The club will take action, you feel what I'm telling you?"

She was in the middle of a full-blown tear fest as I spoke the words in a scathing tone to her. "I'm s-sorry. I really thought, um-"

I cut her off before she could spew more of her bullshit. "If I wanted you here, I would have fuckin told you where to go. I didn't. You followed me like a stalker to get that information, and that's concerning as hell."

She jerked back, wide-eyed, like I'd just slapped her with my hands instead of my words. "No! I'm not, I wasn't. I just, I'm sorry, it won't happen again." She turned then, and damn near ran for the Mustang that was parked out by the road. I snapped a picture of it with my phone so that I had evidence of her being there, and what car she was driving now. None of her ordeal phased me, not her tears, watching her run away, or seeing her peel her high heels off of her feet after she tripped while running. I simply didn't give a shit about her. At least, I didn't until I turned back to see Poppy's eyes dart from where Julie had finally made it inside her car and back to me. Then she glared at her brother too.

"That was not okay." Poppy turned and went back inside, slamming the door behind her as she did so. I turned to Smoke as the bastard began to chuckle and I growled out my response to him.

"What the fuck am I supposed to do about that?" I hissed low so my voice wouldn't carry as I pointed to the door that had just been slammed on the both of us.

Chief being Chief moved over to his bike and grabbed two plastic grocery bags full of food out of the saddlebags.

He held them up triumphantly. "Maybe food will be the way to her heart. I just happened to bring some with me. As if on cue, by the time he got back to the door, it opened. It only opened a sliver though so I couldn't even get a look at Poppy on the other side.

"You brought food?" she asked Chief.

"You going to invite me in to eat with you guys or slam the door in my face again?" The door opened wider to admit him into the house. Just as I was stepping up to the stoop it slammed closed again. She slammed the damn door in my face. I couldn't believe it. Stunned, I glanced back out to the street where the Mustang was now missing, and I shook my head. I could believe it. I'd be pissed as all hell if the situation were reversed and her ex-husband – husband actually – came walking up to the house making demands. Even if I knew it wasn't her fault, it would still take me a while to process that fact. I sat on the stoop and decided to wait. I knew I still had club business to attend to with Ghost, and a call to make to Angel Girl about Shep's family, but right now, my woman was going to be my priority.

It took a few minutes for the door to open again. When it did, I stood immediately and looked her in the eyes as I spoke. "You're right to be mad. My shit hit your doorstep, and that is not okay. You have to understand that I agree with you. It is abso-fuckin-lutely not okay. I will deal with Julie to make sure this never happens again."

"I think you already did that," she told me, and then just stood there for a few minutes watching me. Finally, I attempted to clear my throat so I could get out a better apology for shit I had absolutely no control over, but she beat me to it. "I'm sorry. I know you couldn't help the fact that she just showed up with all of her assumptions. That doesn't mean I don't feel the things I do. I needed a moment to get myself together."

"I know," I agreed. "I promise, we'll get everything figured out and this won't be an issue moving forward, ever. If someone comes to your doorstep claiming I sent them, I'm a phone call away or you call someone from the club immediately, okay?"

She nodded her head in agreement, and when she didn't say anything else, I figured I had to get the rest out of the way. "I don't have long. I came running when Chief texted, but I'm still in the middle of shit." I hated that I had to walk away again when what we really need to do was talk things out. At the same time, I had other people's lives in my hands. I needed to let Shep know what was going on with his family and give him the option of stepping up and becoming part of the club now that he was knee deep in the worst of the shit we ever faced anyway.

"Go, get back to what you're doing. I've got Brant, and neither of us is going anywhere." I didn't even have anything good to say to that. I wanted to stay there with them, not walk away to handle other people's shit. Then again, it wasn't just other people's shit anymore. The moment those Russian bastards killed my family, it became my problem completely.

I leaned in and kissed her, melding her lips with my own in an embrace that promised more where that came from. I felt her in that kiss. Not just her lips, but the promise of having all of her for myself one day. She was the dream, and damn if I wasn't going to work my ass off to make sure that dream came true.

"We're finishing this later, Poppy, and I'm not just talking about where that kiss was going."

I WAS JUST LEAVING Shep's place when I got a text from Chief.

Chief: Meet me at your place.

Smoke: On the way

No sooner did I have my leg lifting over the bike to get off, than I heard Chief's voice call out to me from a couple feet away. He had clearly been waiting for me in the parking lot instead of upstairs at the apartment.

"You need to pull your head out of your ass, *brother*." He spat the last word like it was something dirty in his mouth. "If you're using my sister as some sort of convenience, part-time fuck and babysitter for your nephew, you need to knock that shit off right the fuck now!"

"What the fuck did you just say to me?" I yelled and didn't wait for an answer. Instead, I launched myself at Chief and knocked his ass directly to the ground. I managed to get a punch in on his ribs before he used the momentum of my punch to flip me over. He quickly assaulted me with three rapid jabs to my right side and then one hard-core punch to my right that damn near knocked the wind out of me. I felt something snap in there, but knew it wasn't going to be anything more than a hairline fracture. I'd broken my ribs before. It would heal, but I was going to make the mother-fucker pay for the pain he just heaped on me.

"She's it for me, you stupid fuck!" I yelled at him as I gave as good as I got.

"She's not a fucking toy!" He snarled as he pounded on me some more, trying to get the drop on the rib he knew he already cracked. I kept it protected and nailed him in the eye hard enough that his head was spinning and I was able to flip him over and gain control again.

"She is the fucking love of my life and you ever disrespect her by talking that way about her again, and this will look like a walk in the fuckin' park, you hear me?"

Chief started chuckling then, despite the hurt I was putting on him. "That's all I needed to hear," he declared and then brushed me off of him like I was nothing and stood up to offer his hand to help me up too. I declined his help and stood on my own two feet. I will admit, I winced a bit as the movement jarred my throbbing rib.

"Feel better now? Get all that aggression that's been riding you so hard out of your system for a while?" Chief asked me.

I nodded at him, acknowledging what I knew he was trying to convey. It wasn't so much the work I was putting into finding my sister's killer that was eating at me and keeping me from finding my way home to Poppy and Brant so many times now. It was the need to feel control over it all. To break something because I was fucking devastated at losing my sister. I needed the vengeance because all of it was sealed up tight like a powder keg waiting to explode.

"Good, now go home and love my sister the right way." He thought better of it then. "Actually, come back to the clubhouse first. I'll wrap those ribs up, so she doesn't see you gimping around and favoring them like a baby. Knowing Poppy, she'll point the finger my way first and ask questions later."

I laughed at the man, knowing he was afraid of his sister's reaction to getting into a physical altercation with me. I'd have to remember that, because it was sure to be used to my advantage at a later date.

13. GO HOME

THE LAST THING I EXPECTED TO WALK INTO WHEN I FINALLY PULLED my head out of my ass after the row I'd had with Chief was Poppy and Walker going at it in the clubhouse in front of everyone gathered like it was nothing.

"What exactly do you want, Walker? Did you bring signed divorce papers?"

"What? No, Poppy, I don't want the damn divorce. I understand you were mad, but you've had time to cool off and realize how hard things were on me. Yeah, I should have handled things differently, but I was under a lot of stress and you..."

Poppy didn't let him finish. She turned to walk away from him, but must have been filled with rage because she didn't seem to see anything. My woman didn't even notice me standing in the doorway, shocked as shit that this was going down. How the fuck was this asshole here and no one in the Georgia Chapter thought to give us a head's up that he was coming? They better not have given someone a head's up and they didn't pass that information on to me.

"Wait, where are you going? We're in the middle of talking," he shouted at her. I nearly came undone and flew after him then, but Surfer's hand came out and caught hold of my arm.

"You might want to wait on that and see how this place out first, brother."

"What's that supposed to mean?" I asked.

"Not what you're thinking. She won't think too kindly of you butting in right now, though, trust me."

When I glanced back over, Poppy was facing off with the asshole. "You have the audacity to come here, demand to see me, and then tell me about how hard *your* life was and how the stress you were under caused you to fall dick first into every whore at the clubhouse, never check on your wife, or do any goddamn thing for her either? You had it so hard because you couldn't do simple tasks the doctors asked you to do in order to get your sperm count up like wear different underwear.

"Yeah, I can see how that demand made you run straight to other pussy to prove what a man you are. Don't you dare stand here and try to trivialize this shit. You are a grown ass man who made dumbass decisions and now, as a result, the woman who once loved you with everything she had doesn't want you anymore. Guess what? It's time to suck it up, and reap what you've sown, because I'm done. I've been done and I don't ever want to go backwards."

"Poppy, I know you were mad. I get it. I fucked up. I know I did, but I'm here now. I pulled my head out of my ass, and-"

She cut him off, obviously as tired of his excuses as I was. "Stop right there. Even if you had managed to pull your head out of your ass – which I highly doubt considering the first thing I saw when I walked in here was some other woman touching you and you doing nothing to stop it – you're still forgetting the part where I said I'm done."

"You don't have to be done. We can work through this. We still love one another. I'll find a way to give you the baby you want, I swear it!"

Poppy growled out her frustrations so loudly the entire place went silent. I've never understood a room being so quiet you could hear a pin drop before, but in that moment, I got it. Everyone tuned into what was going on now.

"I do not still love you. I love someone else. I already have my own baby on the way, and it's not yours!" She yelled, stunning the shit out of me.

She had what? I glanced over at Surfer to see if he heard the same thing I did. He simply nodded and smiled at me.

"You gonna raise another man's baby?" She laughed a sickeningly, humorless laugh. "Never mind, that's a moot point, because even if you were man enough to agree to that, I don't want you to. I can't count on you to be there for me during a goddamn storm, I sure as hell couldn't count on you to be there for sleepless nights, teething, vomiting, and any other thing that might inconvenience your life. I am happy here. I am in love with someone, and that someone isn't you. He's the father of my baby. Now, do you understand? There's nothing left of us. It's all gone, and what little bit had been left before I moved here, you trashed and threw away with your actions."

I wasn't waiting by the doorway any longer. My woman didn't need this shit, especially if what she'd just admitted was true. The last thing she needed while pregnant was this asshole adding to the stress she was already under with taking care of my nephew, me being gone so much, and all the shit brewing with the club. That didn't even touch on her being in a place that was still new to her and trying to establish work clientele to help pay her bills. I moved right up behind her and watched as the asshole gave me a funny look before returning his attention to Poppy.

"You're pregnant?" he asked her for clarification.

I ignored the jackass's question, as did Poppy. "We'll talk about that revelation later at home, but honey, I need you to know, I love you, too." I whispered into her ear before placing a sweet kiss there to follow my words as I reached around her and cupped low on her belly holding the baby I'd somehow managed to put there. Walker didn't miss any of that, and I could see his anger building as his face took on a beet-red tone, his chest heaved, and his shoulders puffed up as his fists clenched at his sides.

"You're my brother!" he yelled. "You knocked up my wife?"

"Ex-wife," I taunted.

"Those papers aren't signed yet," Walker tried to argue.

I made a tsking noise in my throat that I knew he could hear as I rolled my eyes at the man. "She just told you all the ways you screwed up, all the reasons she didn't want you back, and that she was happy, finally. She signed the papers already. In her eyes, in her mind, you two aren't together.

She's just waiting for you and the law to catch up with everything."

"Club first," Walker called out, glancing around the clubhouse briefly, as if looking for the rest of our brothers to back his claim over mine. That shit would not happen in this clubhouse. First, Poppy's family was a club brother here, and he didn't want her anywhere near Walker. Second, our club president loved Poppy and would see to whatever made her happy. Third, these were my brothers. We may have been from the same club, but this was my clubhouse – and wrong or not – they would stand by me. As predicted, no one came to his defense.

"Yeah, we all know you put the club first, every aspect of it, including catering to the whores. That seemed to be your problem. I don't regret making Poppy mine, or anything that resulted from that decision. Best damn woman I've ever met, and I'd be a fool to let her go. You didn't hang on to a good thing, and now you're seeing that, but it's too late. I suggest you get gone back to Georgia, and do something for someone other than yourself for a change, and sign those damn papers."

The asshole ignored me and turned his full attention on Poppy. "I wouldn't care," he pleaded with her. The fucker was seriously begging to get hit.

Poppy laughed at him again. "Yes, you would. The thing is, that part doesn't even matter, because I'm happy right now. I wasn't before. I meant it when I said I wasn't willing to go backwards for anyone, Walk. Not even you."

"Poppy, I promise you I'll get it right this time," he

pleaded. I felt my woman squirm beneath my fingers, and for a brief second, I wondered if she was giving in to him, but I chose to trust in her and see where this went just like Surfer had suggested moments ago.

"How long, Walk?" she asked him point blank.

The confused frown on his face meant he was just as stupid as I thought he was. "What do you mean? How long? I plan on loving you forever, just like I said when we got married."

"No, how long were you fucking other people?" I felt the subtle flinch in her muscles as she asked the question. I don't think she showed any outward sign of how much it hurt to demand that clarification. I also didn't think she really needed to the know the answer, but I knew she was trying to prove a point to him. She wouldn't back away from doing it, even if it hurt her because she needed everything to really sink in for the punk.

Walker looked like he was about to shit himself as he stared at her, face going pale. He fidgeted with the edges of his kutte briefly and wasn't able to look my woman in the eye, let alone answer her question.

"You won't even answer her?" I finally asked, calling the bastard out on his cowardice. "You can't come clean, but you expect her to believe you care enough to stick with her now?" I continued, knowing I was goading him into answering even as I did it.

"Four years," he spat out at me, clearly forgetting for a minute that Poppy was standing there as she sucked in a gasping breath at the truth he admitted to. Then his guilty eyes travelled back down to hers. I knew she had mentioned they were trying for nearly five years to have a baby, so that had to have been a tough blow for her to take. That meant he was fucking around nearly the entire time they'd been trying. I never wanted to knock a mother fucker out more than I did in that moment.

"We were trying to have a baby then, and you were off fucking other people?" she asked as she stared him down.

"Sex was becoming a chore with you, Pop. It was so important to get the baby as a result, but there was no fun in it anymore, because it was like going to work. You know? Something you have to do and not necessarily something you like doing."

What a douchebag. There was no way sex with Poppy could ever be considered a chore. Hell, I'd have made it my life's mission to try every position possible, and damn near fuck her to death until she had my kid inside of her if that was what she wanted. This asshole didn't deserve her, and hell, maybe he knew that, too. The problem had been he was too much of a fucking pussy to let her go to someone who did.

"You do realize that you having sex with other people was probably why you kept failing to get me pregnant in the first place, so you literally perpetuated your own problem and made the situation worse?"

"I didn't," he started to say, and we all watched as the reality of what he'd done finally started to sink in. I never had an infertility issue before, but from what Poppy had talked about, storing up the baby batter for a person with a low sperm count was key to successfully making a baby happen. If he'd been out there fucking around all that time, he was blowing off load after load with other women, and by doing so he fucked over any chances they could have had.

I scoffed at that thought but spoke the rest out loud for him to hear. "Like I said, you're an idiot."

"Well, I think we're done here," Poppy finally stated before she turned and patted in my arms and patted my hand to signal I needed to let her go. I wouldn't begrudge her the space she probably needed.

"Poppy," Walker called out to her once more, sounding more desperate than ever and clearly realizing there was no going back from that. I let Poppy go and stood between him and her retreating back.

"No! If you hadn't fucked up bad enough before, you have to know that there's no coming back from that. You don't come back from that kind of bullshit with a woman like Poppy."

"She's only walking away out of obligation since you fucking knocked her up. We have a love that lasts a lifetime." He sounded so sure of himself that I couldn't help myself when I burst out laughing.

"Like I said, you're an idiot. You may have had a love that would have lasted a lifetime if you'd cherished it, nurtured it, and not fucked around on it. You had to know she wouldn't put up with that shit. You knew what you were doing. Not only were you betraying her, but you were single-handedly ensuring that her dream never came true. She may have loved you at one time, but you never could have loved her. That's not something you do to someone you love. You don't shit on their dreams while betraying them and expect that they'll still be there to make you feel better about yourself. You fucked up, *brother*." I spat the last word out at him because I definitely didn't feel a club obligation to the bastard.

"You fucked up, and now you get to spend the rest of your life living with that decision. What you don't get to do is try to force yourself back on that woman after you broke every bit of love she had for you. You did that. Got no one to blame but yourself." I started walking away before I turned back to look at the sorry bastard one more time. "She's mine now, and I'm not stupid, fucker. She ain't never coming back to you."

"Just wait, you'll screw up, too, because she's too damn perfect for any of us," he muttered.

"No, she was just too perfect for you since you couldn't see what you had. Now, tuck your tail and go home." I turned and went left the way Poppy and Chief had gone earlier only to walk into the middle of their conversation.

"...tell Smoke first, but every time I tried something happened. I found out when I got home from Pittsburg, and then everything happened with Smoke's family."

"Jesus, talk about bad timing."

"Exactly. Then every time I've attempted to tell him he's had to run off or something has happened to make me put it on the back burner," she managed to tell her brother.

"We're going to talk about that when we get somewhere private," I said to her without announcing my presence in any other way.

"Smoke," she tried to chime in, but I didn't let her. Too

much of our personal shit had been played out for the club before we were even able to discuss it. I needed to get her home and fucking chill with my family while we discussed what our future was going to look like. Not that I needed a conversation to know that I wanted our future to be together.

"Let's get Brantley, and get back to your house before we talk about anything else, okay?"

"Okay," she agreed. Then she smiled so sweetly at me that it took everything I had in me not to just strip her down right there and show her how much she belonged to me.

I held out my hand to her, but just as we were about to leave, Ghost came in and eyed me. "A minute before you go?"

"Shit," I nodded and shook my head as I looked at Poppy who was clearly disappointed by the change of plans.

"He won't be but a few minutes behind you darlin'," Ghost told her. She smiled and then left while Chief stood there glaring at both Ghost and I. I couldn't say that I blamed him.

Once Poppy had cleared the room, Chief moved up into my face and pointed a finger at me. "Don't fuck up. Remember our little chat and make sure you actually get home to her tonight." He turned a glare on Ghost. "No matter what he has to say. The man should know better than to distract you right this minute after the bomb that was just dropped out there."

Ghost at least had the good sense to look guilty. "What's going on?"

"I just," he started, then ran his fingers through his dirty blond hair he'd recently trimmed. "Shit. I'm sorry. I shouldn't have stopped you. It can wait. I wanted to make sure you were okay, and knew that you have Cedar Falls support with what's happening between you and Poppy. I know it's not ideal when another brother steps in and picks up a woman who was already claimed by someone else in the club, but I needed you to know that we all support you. This isn't a normal situation, and we all know that the two of you belong together and that little fucker treated her like second-hand shit. Besides, it's her opinion that I'm factoring here, and she made it pretty clear out there. I just wanted you to know that I've already put the call in to Sweet and let him know where his man really went."

"I appreciate all of that."

The guilty look swamped his face again before he managed to look up at me once more. "I think you should take some time and spend it with your family. That dynamic has changed quite a bit in the past week alone, and this hunt that we're on is already taking its toll. Hell, we all heard Poppy, and saw your reaction. You didn't know before she got pissed enough to blurt it out." I started to interrupt him, but he staved off my words. "I know better than anyone how fleeting our time with our families can be and the precarious rope they sometimes rest on. Don't make the mistakes I did. Don't make your own, equally devastating, ones either. You told Walker out there that you aren't stupid. Prove it. Take some time and be with your woman."

"What if me taking my time to be with her means we let someone slip through the cracks and they come for her next?" Ghost winced at that question. "Our time isn't a given, but I can damn sure work to prolong it. She knows why it's important, and the quicker we get this done, the easier our lives will be. I appreciate the sentiment and you looking out for us, but I can't just step back and not take these fuckers out when we find them."

"I figured you'd say that," he huffed out in frustration. "Hell, I can't preach it, because I wouldn't step back either. Bender was my brother. Soph and little man were family too." He shook his head and I watched as the man's eyes misted over. "We'll do whatever it takes to see those fuckers pay for taking them from us. Now, go on and get out of here before your woman gets pissed at me." He grinned up at me as he casually wiped at the moisture that threatened to spill out of his eyes and give his emotions away. "I'm a little terrified of her, truth be told." He grinned up at me then.

"As we all should be. Walker was right about one thing, she's too good for any of us, but damn if I'm the idiot who will walk away." Nothing more needed to be said so it was time to get my ass back to Poppy's house and relieve whichever prospect had been charged with following her when she walked out the door.

When I made it back to Poppy's place, I watched through the window at first as she laughed at something Brantley had said. Brant was lying beside Bubba on the floor playing with his blocks while the dog looked happy to just be watching as the little boy knocked down whatever he'd been building and squealed with glee. It brought everything home for me. That one little picture of life without me in it. They could be happy. They could move on and forget that I was supposed to be there. Not that I thought they wanted to, but the thing was, the assholes who were responsible for killing my family needed to be brought down and soon. I needed it behind me, so I didn't miss any more of these moments than I had to for my day job. I needed them gone because nothing was going to threaten the happiness of the people inside these walls. Resolving myself to the fact that I'd have to sacrifice a little more time from them now to make that happen, I knew the hard sell would be to Poppy once I got inside. I also knew it was time to start house hunting. We couldn't all fit in Poppy's place, and the apartment I had was not exactly pet friendly for a massive dog like Bubba.

Letting myself in using the key Poppy had given me, it only took a second before Brantley was calling out to me.

"Unc Moke, wook what I made."

"That's really cool, little man!" I leaned down and kissed Brant's head as he smiled his crooked grin at me. Then I flipped his hair and moved toward Poppy. She sat there waiting, and I could see the tension in her shoulders, the worry in her eyes, with each step. That's when I decided direct and to the point was the way I'd need to go with her.

"I get that I have failed to make myself clear with you," I started and watched as the worry grew.

"I thought I was clear, but according to your brother, you're still confused so I'm going to lay it out for you and I need you to hear me." She made the smallest movement of her chin to let me know that I could go on and she was listening. So I did. "I'm with you. Only you. I don't want anyone else, Poppy. I am committed and I honestly don't know how else to say that except that I thought it was straight forward that you were my old lady." Her shocked breath told me I hadn't been clear enough before. What the hell did she think I was playing at all this time? The ridiculous friends with benefits notion she had brought up that first day?

"Don't care that you're still married to some other fool who was too stupid to hang onto the best thing he'd ever get." I scoffed at the memory of my club brother and the fact he had been idiot enough to allow a woman like her to be neglected until the point she no longer loved him. "Better than he deserved, the idiot. You're my old lady, I don't see you any other way."

"Sophie told me you never told anyone that Julie was your old lady. I just thought," I sat beside her and gave her thigh a gentle squeeze. It was enough to stop her in her tracks.

"Julie never was. The difference is, I've already told every single man in the clubhouse and the firehouse that you're mine. They understand that. Now, I need you to understand that I should have made that perfectly clear to you. I'm sorry I didn't do better." She looked like she was about to cry, but I gave her a moment. Poppy needed to absorb exactly what I was telling her. Her divorce still pending didn't matter. We weren't playing games anymore. I wasn't waiting any longer. I'd claimed her, and while she adjusted to the thought of us, I hadn't remembered that she was the most important person who needed to know that.

"Now, tell me our news, because I don't want to think about the way I found out. I want to hear from your lips to my ears like it was meant to be."

"I'm so sorry about that," she apologized. "I got so frustrated earlier, and I just blurted it out. I hadn't even told anyone. Well, Leanne knew, but that's because she was worried I was getting sick a lot."

"See, that's something we're going to discuss, because I feel like a real asshole right now since I didn't know you were still even getting sick."

She reached for me and smoothed her soft hand down my face as if she could wipe my regrets away with a simple touch. Hell, she almost succeeded. "I didn't want you to know." That took the calm she'd managed to sooth into me right the fuck back away. How could she not want me to know about the fact that she'd been sick? "I didn't want you to think there was something wrong until after I knew for sure what was going on. At the same time you had things going on with your family, and when I found out I wanted to tell you right away, but that was the day you guys walked into the clubhouse with bad news."

That made sense and I hated to think that our happy news got delayed because of my family's tragedy, but really what was she supposed to do? I could see where Poppy had been stuck between a rock and a hard place with trying to tell me. I sighed heavily, frustrated with the way the last couple weeks had played out, as well as the lack of resolution. "Then I was constantly running out every time you wanted us to talk." I reminded the both of us why she hadn't been able to tell me since. "I really fucked that up, didn't I?"

"No, you didn't. This hasn't exactly been an easy week for anyone, but especially not for you. I understand. I'm just sorry you found out that way. I'm sorry you weren't the first one I told, because that was how I planned on it happening. I hadn't even told Chief, because I wanted you to know first. I guess everything just hit me all at once and I really wanted it to sink in for Walker that I am never coming back to him."

"You said you were happy. Earlier, when you were talking to him."

Her smile was contagious as she answered me. "I am the happiest I've ever been, which makes me feel horrible at times, because this is such an incredibly inappropriate time for me to feel that way considering your loss, and Brant's loss. I know he doesn't really understand yet, and maybe he won't until many years from now. Still, it's crap timing for me to find my happiness and you to be so lost in grief and driven by revenge."

"Poppy, it's not revenge driving me. I want that too, but mostly I want to make sure that you and Brant are safe, even more so now that I know it's not just the two of you I have to worry about." I moved closer so I could reach over and touch her belly where our child was growing. I was still in awe of the fact that I'd managed to get her pregnant, especially since it was something she'd been trying for so long with her ex. "In case I forgot to say it, I am so damn excited about this." I leaned over further and kissed her still nonexistent baby belly. "I will take good care of all of you, I swear. I will never step out on you. I will never take you for granted. Poppy, you are everything, and if I ever don't treat you like that's exactly what you are, you will kick me in the ass and set me straight, because I can't lose you. Your idiot ex still doesn't realize. Obviously, he thinks he does, but one night soon, he's going to be sitting there with some cheap imitation of you, he's going to hear about how wonderful your life is, and then it's going to click for him that he could have been part of that. I think it's starting to set in for him now, otherwise I doubt seriously he would have offered to raise another man's kid today."

"I don't care what he's going through. He brought it on himself."

"I know that, honey. I'm just saying, you and me, we are never going to get to that point, because I know exactly what I've got right here." I kissed her belly once more before sitting up and facing her again. "When do you need to go see the doctor?"

"Soon. I haven't made an appointment yet, because of the timing of everything else."

"Don't do that. You take care of yourself and our baby above everything, you hear? There are plenty of people who can keep an eye on Brantley while you go to an appointment, and as long as you schedule it for a day I'm not with the firehouse, I'll be there too." I moved my lips to her and placed a gentle kiss there too. "Make no mistake, I want to be there. I want to be there for everything."

"That's good because I want you to be there for everything," she told me just as Brantley decided to make his presence known again and move into Poppy's lap.

"I be der for tings?" Brantley asked looking worried.

"You will always be there for things, lil' man," she told him with a conviction that no one could deny.

His smile was nearly as bright as hers was. "Good. Me likes tings."

I laughed at his response, because there was no telling what was going through his head. "Wonder what he's actually thinking of?"

"Who knows, but if I have anything to say about it, he'll get everything he dreams of."

"You have everything to say about it now," I informed her. She was our family now. Poppy, Brantley, our baby, Bubba, and me. There was no going back. She wanted a family, and she stepped right into one when she met me.

14. FAMILY TIME

BENT OVER THE BED, POPPY SCREAMED INTO THE PILLOW AS I plowed into her from behind. Besides the fact that we hadn't had any alone time when we weren't just dog tired and sleeping, we definitely hadn't had time to enjoy one another lately either, and I was bound and determined to make up for that. I didn't know if it was the time spent apart and appreciation for finally coming together again, her hormones, or what, but Poppy was soaking fucking wet and it was driving me wild. I hadn't wanted to take her from behind like this. I wanted to be able to watch her face as she came apart in my arms, but with Brant right across the hall, and Poppy unable to be quiet during sex, that wasn't an option.

"So wet for me, honey."

She responded though I couldn't understand the words that were muffled by the pillow she was biting into. It didn't matter, because I knew whatever she'd been trying to say had only been encouragement to keep going. I wouldn't disappoint her.

I took a moment to run my fingers gently down her back from the nape of her neck where he hair was swept off to the side all the way down her spine to the crack of her ass. My eyes followed the trail of my fingers as I leisurely stroked in and out of her. I was memorizing her in this moment. The softness of her skin, the way little bumps erupted in the wake of the path my fingers had taken, and the way her hips tilted up just a bit more to urge me on even when she didn't have a voice all settled deep into my soul. The moment locked in place, never to be forgotten before I reached around her and grabbed one of her tits with my right hand while I started stroking her clit with my other. All the while I never changed the tempo of my thrusts even though she attempted to buck against me in order to get me to pick up the pace.

Finally, she turned her head up from the pillow and tossed me a grin from over her shoulder. "If you don't pick up the pace, I'm just going to take a nap, stud! I'm creating another human here, and it's sapping my energy." She winked, letting me know she wasn't tired at all. She was just demanding of my attentions, and what she didn't realize was that she had also just stroked my fucked-up caveman ego. Hell yeah she was making a human. The one I fucked into her, and that was everything.

I picked up my thrust game, giving it to her just a little bit harder each time but maintaining the same overall speed. The little squeaks the movements had her making were music to my ears, but it wasn't until they had become a regular occurrence that I added speed to the harder thrusts too. With each one, her ass would ripple delightfully making me want to lean in and chomp down on that lush ass of hers.

Instead, I angled her hips a little more, and drove home exactly what we'd both been needing. I took her, I gave her all of me, and within minutes, she was screaming my name so loud the pillow could no longer contain it. That was when she tightened up, squeezing the shit out of my cock as she came all over me. I slapped her ass and pinched down on her clit in order to prolong her orgasm as I chased my own. Just before she dropped her chest down as her shaky arms gave out, I was coming inside of her and growling out my own release and rode her body down to the mattress, pulling us into a position where I was the big spoon and she the little while my cock continued to rest inside of her.

"Popwee Otay?" Brant's concerned voice from the hallway had me searching for the covers to throw over Poppy since I couldn't remember if I had locked the door behind us or not.

"I'm okay, baby," she called out to him.

"Whys da door not wocked?"

"It's locked, little man," I told him.

"Unwocks it!" His little demand had us both chuckling. I had tossed Poppy one of my shirts and pulled on a pair of boxer shorts before heading to the door to let the little monster in who had nearly been a major cockblock. Hell, for a brief moment, I wondered if this was why Bender hadn't managed to knock my sister up again, because of his mini-me cock-blocking son. Then, I wanted to throw up, because it hit me that they'd never get a chance to grow their family and they'd probably both gladly give that up to have their son interrupting mommy and daddy's fun times.

"Hey," Poppy called out to me, worry etching her beautiful visage as she watched the thoughts play out across my expressive face. "They would have been thinking the same things," she told me. I knew she was right, because I'd heard Bender joke about how they had to sneak in quickies because his son had sex-dar, as he called it. Radar for when his parents were having sex.

"I know." My voice came out too gruff and thick for my liking.

"Me sweep wit Popwee?" Brant asked, but he wasn't asking me, he was asking her while rubbing his tired eyes. I knew it was going to happen the minute her own sleepy eyes landed on him and I watched her face soften and that sweet smile of hers give all the answer that was needed before Brant climbed up under the covers. Then, the little shit looked right at me as he grabbed hold of her arm and pulled it around him so that she was now the big spoon to his little. I swear, I saw triumph in his eyes like the little shit just stole my woman. I looked heavenward and promised Bender and my sister retribution one day. I knew this was their payback for all the times I laughed about how interruptive their son was in their sex lives.

I left them to it and took Bubba outside one last time. When we came back in, he went straight to Brant's room and whined because the little boy wasn't tucked up in his bed. I just shook my head and laughed. "I see he already rules this house," I grumbled. I didn't honestly mind though. "Come on, Bubba. He's in with Poppy." As if the dog understood, he moved past me before I could even turn and made himself at home beside the bed where Brant had a hand and a foot dangled over the edge, and my woman's arm still slung around him. I crawled in behind her and managed the most peaceful night of sleep I'd had since before my family was torn apart.

My cell would not stop vibrating on the nightstand so finally, I rolled over and answered it at the same moment I realized Poppy, Brant, and Bubba were no longer in the room. "Yeah?"

"Smoke, just checking in with you. Everything good?" Ghost's voice sounded worn down and I wondered how much longer the man was going to keep up with being club president. He'd seen his share of club drama over the years, and keeping the men together was something that took a toll on a person.

"I'm good. Shit, what time is it?" I pulled the phone away from my ear as I heard him chuckle. "Almost 11?" There was no way I'd slept in until almost 11 in the morning. Shit, it was almost lunch time.

"I take it you slept well?" Ghost managed to get out amidst his laughter.

"Fuck! I guess I did. You have something for me? If not, I need to get up and join the land of the living. I'm supposed to be here making shit easier on Poppy, not sleeping while she carries on as usual."

"You need down time too, brother. You've been going hard. Actually, that's what I wanted to tell you. We're running down a few leads the electronic way, and I want you to take time off from club shit for a couple days. We need you fresh when we get the information and everything's a go."

"Do not sit on anything thinking I need to recharge!" It was a demand, and I didn't care in that moment whom I was speaking with either. I meant it. There would be hell to pay if they kept a lead from me, thinking I needed to recharge, and the bastards were able to go to ground. I'd be equally pissed if they took off and went after them without me.

"Don't worry, Smoke. Nothing is happening without you there, and we sure as fuck aren't going to be sitting on anything. Soon as we know, you'll get the call."

"Fine." I huffed the word out and then scratched a hand down the beard that had been threatening to grow in fully. "That it?"

"That's it. Go enjoy family time while you have it, brother."

"Yeah," I told him and then hung up.

By the time I managed to get myself cleaned up and out to the living room, I found Brantley sitting there trying to explain to Bubba why he couldn't build with his blocks. Poppy was in the kitchen making what looked like lunch. I moved right up behind her and put my hands around her waist, resting them gently on her belly before I dipped down and placed a kiss on her neck. She had her hair swept up into some sort of messy bun-ponytail hybrid. It probably would have looked horrible on anyone else, but not Poppy. Her green eyes flared at me as she turned to offer up one of her brilliant smiles.

"Did you sleep well?" she asked, as if that was necessary. Obviously, I had.

"Too well, apparently. I didn't mean to miss breakfast with you guys. You should have woken me."

She turned in my arms and shook her head at me before running a finger under my eye and smoothing it out across my cheek until she reached the short beard I'd just trimmed up. "No. You needed some good sleep for once. I was happy to let you sleep and get rested. Now that you're up though, you could get Brant ready so we can go have a picnic. That's what he wanted for lunch."

My heart slammed against my chest. Poppy couldn't have known, but Brant had been on his way to a picnic with his parents when the crash happened. That was their thing. They'd go off to find another new place where there were easy hiking trails, or something to see in nature like a water-fall or a river, and they'd take a family day to go picnic and enjoy being in the world without being surrounded by the day-to-day bullshit.

"I'm not sure that's a wise thing to do," I told her.

"Why not? It's just a picnic." I took a minute to explain things to her and watched as her face morphed into one of sadness when she glanced back into the living room where Brant was still playing while Bubba kept watch over him.

"I didn't know," she finally said.

"You couldn't have known that's what he was asking for."

Her shoulders immediately straightened, and she tipped her chin up to me. "We're giving him this. From now until he's a grown man, we're going to give him that part of his family so he can always have a piece of them. His memories will fade, but the tradition they started doesn't have to."

I didn't think it was possible to love her any more than I already did, but damn, she was amazing. "Okay, Poppy. We'll do this, but until these assholes are caught and brought to justice, we're going to have to make a modified picnic." I leaned in and kissed her nose before I took off for the hall closet where Poppy kept spare blankets and sheets.

"What are you doing?"

"I'm preparing a special magical place to have a picnic. You make the rest of that food, and I'll get everything else ready."

There was an old area rug tucked away in the tiny little shed off to the side of the house that was perfect for what I'd need, and once I was finished, I had managed to string up a nice little blanket fort that Poppy would be able to stand up straight in, even if I had to duck down a bit. Little man would think it was huge. When I was finished, I went back inside and gathered up my family while helping Poppy bring the last of our picnic supplies out.

"Whoa!" Brant's eyes lit up when he saw the outside of the fort. Granted, it was nothing more than a bunch of mismatched sheets, but still in a kid's eyes it was something new and shiny. "What this?"

"It's a magic fort, little man."

"Whoa!" His response had us both grinning as he entered. I had built in a little entryway to the big tented room, but once we got in there I dropped to my knees and put down the plate of sub sandwiches Poppy had made. I had laid the area rug out on the ground and then piled blankets and pillows all around the periphery, so it looked like we were in the middle of genie's lamp or something. Brant moved in circles, taking everything in and then he ran to me and threw his arms around my neck. "Unc Moke, you builded dis fo me?"

"Yeah, buddy."

"Wub you," he told me before letting go and calling out to Bubba who had been hesitant about entering our little blanket fort. "Bubsba!" He demanded and finally Bubba low-crawled his way into the tent as we laughed at the beast of a dog who looked like he was afraid of his own shadow when confronted with the monstrosity of sheets in the yard where he usually did his business and played catch.

"I think Bubba's wondering what we did to his yard," I told Brant. He laughed.

"Bubsba, come. Wets pway."

"How about we eat first and then play?" Poppy asked.

"Bubsba has a sub, too?"

"I have something special for Bubba," Poppy insisted, and she pulled a large rawhide bone out of the little backpack she had brought out. Once Bubba had it, he took off to a far corner and lay there while gnawing at the thing. Seeing Bubba content made Brantley more willing to eat first and play later.

It didn't take long for little man to finish his food and go about exploring the tent space I'd created. It wasn't even long after that when both Bubba and Brantley were out like a light for nap time. There was something to be said for having the pillows splashed all around the place.

"Look at that, didn't even have to fight him into a bed. Maybe we should leave this up all the time," Poppy mused.

I snickered. Considering not a single bit of this is water-proof I don't think that will work out too well."

She shrugged. "Worth the shot."

"Has he been hard to get down for naps?" I felt bad again because she'd been dealing with that while I'd been mostly absent.

"It's not that bad, but he doesn't like to go to sleep because he has bad dreams."

"Shit, Poppy" I started to say but she leaned over and put a finger to my lips.

"Shh, it's okay. Everything is going to be okay. It was bound to happen with him. He lived through a horrific car accident that killed both of his parents. He's adjusting to them no longer being here. I'd say he's doing remarkably well, considering."

I could have apologized a thousand times over for leaving it all to her, but I knew she didn't want to hear that. Instead I leaned in, moved her finger away from my mouth and replaced it with her lips instead. "Thank you," I whispered against them. "Thank you for being there for both of us."

"You never have to thank me for that, Smoke. I know why you haven't been around. I understand. If I'd been able to blame someone for my family's death, I'd be doing the same thing."

"No, you wouldn't. Your brother would," I corrected. She simply laughed.

"If that's what you need to keep telling yourself. If someone had been responsible, I would have just joined up with all the girls of S.H.E. and rode off into the sunset with them to get my vengeance."

"You know how to ride a bike?" I asked while grinning down at her.

"Well, no. It can't be that hard though. I'm sure one of them would have been able to teach me."

"I'll teach you. Never know when those crazy bitches will want to expand and start a new chapter." I winked at her then and she just laughed at me.

"Keep grinning like you know I won't do it. I'll be the most badass motorcycle momma you've ever seen!" Her instance was cute as hell.

"Speaking of," I told her as I managed to get Poppy spread out beneath me on her back. "I think you're going to have to hold off on your plans of female biker world domination until this little bundle arrives." I nudged her belly, through her shirt, with my nose before leaning back up and kissing her again. "If I didn't tell you before, I need for you to know, I'm so fucking happy to be starting a family with you."

"Me too," she breathed out before our lips locked in a lingering kiss once more.

15. CLUB BUSINESS

THE GIANT GRIN ON MY FACE AS I WALKED INTO THE FIREHOUSE TWO days after seeing my baby on that monitor couldn't be missed. "What the hell is that all about?" Shep asked skeptically. Surfer just smiled as he watched me approach them. He already knew about the little bomb Poppy had dropped in the clubhouse.

Instead of telling either of them my news I held up the small black and white photo of the blob the doc told me was my kid. "This," I explained as I watched Shep's eyes round out in surprise while Surfer simply continued to smile at me.

"Congrats, brother!" Surfer finally offered up with a quick hug and slap on the bag once I was close enough.

"Are you serious?" Shep asked while eyeing the ultrasound photo. "Poppy?"

"Who the fuck else?" I asked, brows knitting together in confusion with a slight twinge of anger.

"Sorry man. I saw Julie at the funeral. She was awful

clingy, didn't know if there was something you weren't telling me."

"Fuck no!" I roared before Shep threw his hands up in the air and backed up a few steps.

"Bring it back down, dude," Surfer told me. "Honest mistake," he added. Not that it helped much. I knew I was overreacting, but the idea of someone close to me not knowing that I wouldn't step out on Poppy pissed me the fuck off.

That was when Shep damn near tackle-hugged me. "'Bout time we had some good news around here. I'm so fuckin' happy for you, man."

"Thanks," I mumbled into his shoulder before pushing him off of me. "You know it's not your baby, right?" I teased him. "We're not having a love child. That shit was over the top."

He came at me with arms out again. "But baby cakes! You said you loved me! What the fuck do you mean it's not my baby?" I took off in the opposite direction with the asshole chasing me. "Come on honey bunch, bring that baby belly to me so I can love on it!"

"What in the absolute hell is going on out here?" We all pulled up short when our Captain's voice rang out through the engine bay.

"It's nothing. Smoke's having Shep's baby, but won't admit it." I watched as our Captain rolled his eyes and then reached down to pick something up off the floor. Shit, how had I not noticed we dropped the ultrasound photo? I made my way to him with my grabby hands already reaching out.

"This yours?" he asked.

"Yes, sir!"

He smiled widely at me then. "Tell Julie congrats for me."

"Here we go again!" I heard Surfer huff out as he moved in close. Obviously, I needed to bring Poppy around the station so everyone knew I had a new woman.

"Broke it off with that bitch almost eight months ago," I told the man. "Poppy is my woman. She's the one who's pregnant." I heard a gasp behind us and finally looked to see why my Captain had assumed things. In an unfuckingbeliev-able turn of events, Julie was standing there by Engine One watching us.

"What the hell are you doing here? I thought I made myself crystal fucking clear when you fucking stalked me and showed up at Poppy's house trying to snatch Brantley?"

"She what?" Shep yelled from across the bay where I'd left him.

"I wasn't trying to snatch him," she insisted. "I thought it was what you would want."

"Why the fuck would I want that when I told you I was through with you and not to come around me again?"

"We talked at the cemetery."

"No, you talked and clung to me. Your bullshit made me miss my own sister's funeral. I wasn't able to lay her to rest with my mom's necklace because you caused a huge fuckin' scene. Why the hell would I want you to pick up my nephew?"

"Oh God!" Her voice trembled, along with her quivering lip, indicating that she was about to full-blown emotional meltdown. It was something I refused to deal with.

"You need to get the fuck out of here and don't come

back. I'll be talking to the magistrate later about a fucking restraining order against you for Poppy, Brant, and me."

"There's no need," she offered dejectedly. "I just came to tell you I was sorry. I thought..." She shook her head as tears fell down her face. "I thought we were never over and that you just needed time."

"I have an old lady who I'm proud to put on the back of my bike and claim," I insisted knowing it was a low blow since I'd never publicly claimed her as such. "We're starting a family together. You need to stay gone."

"How could you replace me like that? We were together for five years, and you never claimed me that way."

"Maybe because somewhere in the back of my mind I knew you were being a deceitful cunt. You were too busy pining for my brother to care if I fucking claimed you properly, remember?"

"That was only early on," she argued again.

"I'm not having this conversation with you again. We are done. Been done. Retroactively done. If I could take back four years of memories of being with you, I would. I'd keep the first year though, as a reminder of what a lying bitch you are. Now, get the fuck out of here."

"Sounds like we can call our boys in blue since she's been an ongoing problem," one of the guys mentioned. I wasn't sure which because I was physically radiating anger at that point.

"I'm sorry. I didn't mean..." she sniffled loudly. "Oh God, I'm so sorry," she murmured again before she left, shoulders shaking and hands swiping up to clear away the tears that were streaming down her face. It wasn't that I didn't have a heart to care about someone in pain, but I couldn't bring myself to do so for her. She had caused this. She'd caused a rift between my brother and me that only compounded the problems we were now having after losing Sophie.

"What the fuck is wrong with that woman?" Shep hissed out once she finally made her way out of the engine bay.

I just shook my head. "I don't know what the hell she's thinking lately. I went months without seeing or hearing from her at all, then Soph, and..." I couldn't finish. Just the fact that the bitch would take advantage of my sister's death to try to reinsert herself into my life made me want to punch something or someone. "I need to find these Russian assholes soon. Need an outlet!" My fists clenched at my sides as I tried to unclench my jaw. "I need this shit to be over with so I can get back to life with Poppy, especially now that we have Brantley and a baby on the way too."

Surfer clapped me on my shoulder. "We'll get you there."

I glanced over at him then. "You have your own shit going on right now too," I reminded him. When a guilty looked slipped over his face, I cut those thoughts right off for him. "We never know when shit will hit the fan, brother. You couldn't foresee this shit going down with Gillian and her ex any more than the rest of us could see what happened when we..." Surfer's new woman had a kid already when they met. The kid's father happened to be a member of a rival club, and while he hadn't been in their lives since before she gave birth to Kade, the bastard was trying to force his way back into their lives now that he discovered she was hooking up with an Aces High member.

"When they stuck their necks out for my family and it cost them, heavily," Shep muttered before walking away.

I sighed. Surfer leaned in. "There's no taking his guilt away. He just needs time to come to grips with how everything played out."

"Eat those words, because the same applies to you. You need help with the situation you're in, you just let me know."

"Thanks, dude. Same offer stands," he insisted. Then the serious vibe melted away replaced with happiness. "Tell me about the appointment you went to?"

"We could hear the heartbeat," I managed to get out without getting myself all choked up in my girly fucking emotions. "Sounded like a damn racehorse galloping away in there."

"Yeah? I've heard it before, but I bet that sound is something else when you know it's your kid making it."

"Fuck, I didn't even realize I wanted kids of my own until I met her. Figured I'd already practically raised my brother and sister and didn't need to experience that again."

"You think you'll have more after this?"

"I'm gonna give that woman a whole house full of babies to take care of. Just in case she ever thinks of leaving me, she won't be able to with all those mouths to feed." I explained with a laugh. I didn't have any concern that Poppy would leave me. I just wanted to make sure she was always happy enough that the thought never occurred to her and I knew one way to achieve that was to give her the family she'd been dreaming of for so long.

We spent the rest of our shift moving from a small house fire to three separate accidents with injuries in the surrounding area. By the time we got back to the station with an hour left to go I was ready to crash, but my cell rang curtailing plans of a quick catnap before heading home to my woman and my nephew.

"Yeah?"

"Smoke, gonna need you to get on over to the clubhouse when your shift is over," Ghost demanded.

"You have something?" I asked, knowing it had to be about the Russians, otherwise he'd never bother me at the end of a shift.

"Yeah, brother. We found their rathole and have eyes on them until we can get there."

"Fuck!" I glanced around wondering if I could possibly scoot out early, but the alarm sounding suddenly took that thought away. "Fuck!" I shouted into the phone again.

"We aren't rolling without you, get the job done, then we'll go get the other job taken care of."

"Right," I replied as I hung up and ran to jump back into my gear.

"They're trying to kill us tonight," one of the men grumbled.

"Grab some caffeine on your way, ladies!" I shouted to everyone. "They don't get any easier because we're tired!" That was the truth, because it would be three more hours before I would be able to head to the clubhouse thanks to the fire that took longer to put out than it should have.

WHEN I ROLLED up to the clubhouse, Ghost already had the men on their bikes and ready to go. Tuck, Wren, BigMac, Shorty, Phoenix, and Chief were all geared up, along with Hold 'Em and the newest prospects, Reefer and Mouth, who were bringing up the rear with the box van just in case we needed to bring presents back to the compound.

"My boy came through," Tuck called out, then snickered. "Actually, it was his woman who found them, but he told me I better give him credit because he didn't want you boys knowing he'd been shown up by a woman – again." Everyone laughed. Normally, I probably would have too, but this wasn't the time for humor. The sweet vengeance I'd been craving was so close I could almost taste it on my tongue.

"I'll send her a care package with a ball gag in it so she can shut him up for a while," I called out as I grabbed the coffee Ghost handed me and downed the damn thing in one go.

"You okay to ride? It's been a long night for you," he suggested.

"I'll be fine. Let's go get shit taken care of."

I had texted Poppy that I had club business to handle after work and wasn't sure when I'd be back. I promised to make shit up to her, but honestly, I was starting to get nervous that she would end up giving up on me before long. We had a couple fantastic days before I needed to pull this last shift. I'd give anything to be going home to do it all over again instead of this, but we'd never be able to have that kind of security until this was finished. I needed for this to be laid to rest with Bender and my sister.

Our route was taking us a longer way to where the assholes were hiding out in plain sight in Goldsboro, North Carolina. What could have been just over a four-hour ride was going to take us just under six so that we could stay off the radar for as long as possible.

"Are you sure about this route?" I asked Wren, impatiently after we first took off. A few years back, we had all upgraded our helmets with Bluetooth capability, and recently upgraded to the Sena 30K. It worked out just fine for our group of 12. The prospects weren't blue-toothed in, so we only had 10 people on comms. It was easy enough for our small group to stay in range too, which meant we could actually talk, plan, and strategize on the way.

"I'm positive. They'd be stupid not to have eyes on the direct route from Cedar Falls to Goldsboro. If we took 77 to 74 and 40 they'd know we were about to ride right up their asses. This way, we come in quiet. Once we get in a little closer, we'll split into smaller groups and come in at several different angles. We should still be within Bluetooth range rolling into their general vicinity minus a few spots where it'll get dicey due to distance."

I knew he wasn't wrong. We'd tested the Bluetooth capabilities thoroughly before. We could get a mile apart if we had ten or more riders hooked in. If we scaled it back to essentials, and gave each team leader comms while keeping everyone else silent, we could stretch it to just under a five mile radius. It wouldn't matter anyway, because by the time we got close enough, we wouldn't be using the comms to talk if we could help it since the signal was easy enough to jack into if you knew to watch for it.

Ghost's voice came over the comms a few minutes later, interrupting my thoughts. "We've been told there are fifteen men on site. That means they'll have us outnumbered. A few of our guys from Sierra High are en route too, but they're further away than we were. Since they got the intel and mobilized first, we should be rolling into town around the same time if everything goes according to plan. They're bringing six men they had to spare with them."

"Six?" I questioned. We had twelve, ten strong not counting the prospects so that evened things up, but still I would have thought they'd have sent more.

"They have shit going down in their own backyard, and a few men are out of town on personal shit," Ghost confirmed.

"Who?" I asked, suddenly worried I may end up shot in the back by one of our own brothers.

"Walker won't be here. He was ordered to stay behind and help clean up the mess he made."

I wanted to laugh. I'd bet money the asshole slept with the wrong man's woman down there and was now causing a boatload of trouble for the club as a result. It didn't matter though. Right now, I had more important things to consider. We knew that there were about fifteen men at the facility we would be raiding, but I wondered if there were going to be any civilians.

"Any civies there?"

"Unclear," was Ghost's response.

"How is it unclear?"

"There may be an underground extension of the place they're using. Quickshot wasn't able to get solid info on that before we rode out."

"That means we could be walking into way more than 15 men," I pointed out.

"It's possible, but unlikely."

'Possible, but unlikely' sounded like a bad plan to me, but one we would all go through with anyway, because I wasn't the only one wanting it to be over and the assholes responsible to be put to ground. After what happened to Bender and Sophie, we all knew that women and children weren't off limit targets for these guys. They'd take them out just to cripple us emotionally before they slaughtered our men. It would work too. When we finally approached Goldsboro, Ghost came back on comms to direct us to our meet point with the Sierra High guys.

"What is this place?" I asked as we rolled up to a small farm on the outskirts of the town. There was a pretty decent sized house with a wide wraparound porch centered on the property, but off to the back right, there was a barn where it appeared our Sierra High guys were loading their bikes.

Sweet, the Sierra High President, walked up to us before anyone could answer. "One of Angel Girl's biker bitches moved here with a boyfriend. She's letting us use the garage to store the bikes. Figured it would be better to take the vans as close as we can get rather than alerting them to the presence of a motorcycle club rolling up on their asses."

I glanced around the property again, not exactly liking this change in plans. Sweet must have noticed. "I swear to you, the chick is legit. She's been with Jamie a long time."

"She must have left S.H.E. if she's out here on her own though," I added for clarification.

He nodded his head. "She's on a break, though she has

been in contact with the women about possibly starting a small chapter of S.H.E. over this way."

"Jesus, lady bikers are branching out, huh?" Wren asked giving Ghost a playful punch in the shoulder. "Taught that girl well."

"Hush your mouth, the way your daughter's growing up, she'll be asking to join them soon."

"That's not even funny," Wren told him and proceeded to hop back on his bike and ignore everyone's laughter as he moved his bike over toward the barn.

"What's that about?" Sweet asked. "Thought he admired Jamie."

"He does. His daughter thinks it's okay to have boyfriends already though," Ghost told us, snickering at the prospect of a biker dad faced with the boyfriend issues.

"You still have more girls coming up," I reminded him.

Ghost paled. "They're not ready for boys yet. Won't be until I'm cold and dead in the ground either." He turned to all of us then to emphasize a point he was about to make. "That shit ain't happening today, boys. We're going to head out and kick some ass. We're not worrying about taking names or prisoners this time. We already know everyone involved is going to be in that building."

"Why don't we just level the fucking thing with explosives then?" Tuck asked.

"We know their biggest source of income right now is coming from trafficking women. If we level that building and find out later that there was a lower level full of innocent captives, how are we all going to feel? It could have been Shep's mom and sister held there. It could be any one of the women in our lives we love, including the ones too young to think about being in that situation. Let's get in, and be watchful, just in case. But while we're there, we show no mercy to those Russian fucks."

"For Bender!" Someone yelled.

"For Soph," I added, only to have everyone chime in that this attack would just be for both Soph and Bender. It was for their son too, because one day we all wanted to be able to look Brantley in the eyes and tell him that we got justice for him, for his family.

16. THE BREACH

Two hours later, we had everyone geared up and ready for war with the Russians. When we got to the closed down manufacturing plant, I immediately saw our biggest hurdle in all of this was going to be in keeping shit quiet. They were holed up in an old manufacturing plant that had been closed down, but the plant was sitting right alongside State Rd. 1915 with nothing keeping nosey people driving by from seeing or hearing what was happening.

I glanced over at Wren as we made our approach, getting as close as we dared in the vans. "Did you know it was situated like this?"

"I knew. We don't really have much choice in the location, brother."

"Shit!"

"This is why we need to get in, take care of business, and get the fuck out of there," he admitted.

"We're going to be lucky if we get in and out without anyone ending up heading to the slammer."

"Let's fucking hope not."

There was a wooded lot that was for sale to the east of the property. We rolled the vans in there and made sure the vehicles were parked with their engines facing out for the quick getaway we were no doubt going to need. We also made sure they were hidden in the trees and the prospects were made to stay with them so that we had someone who could pull up in case we had any wounded we needed to load in quick fashion.

As soon as we had the vans squared away along with the prospects and their orders, the rest of us took off, getting into position as the sun began to set. We had to wait until all of our men were in position. The guys from Sierra High had pulled in the tree-lined lot to the west of the building and were coming in hot from that side. We had a few of our men break off to come in on the rear. We were literally surrounding the building. It was a good thing we did too, because what we hadn't been expecting was that they were loading up their vehicles and ready to head out.

"Delivery bay opened. Looks like they're planning on heading out."

"The fuck you say?" I yelled into my comms. There was no way that was happening. "Prospect, bring van 1 around and block that entrance. You let those fuckers get through you, and you'll never patch in."

"Jesus," Shorty hissed next to me. "Poor prospect is probably pissing his Levi's right about now."

"As long as he does his fuckin' job, I don't care how wet he makes his pants."

"Move in," Ghost called out. "Can't wait any longer." As

soon as we started moving in, it became obvious why it looked like they were about to head out. There was a truck in the bay that hadn't opened yet, and I caught a glimpse inside just before the asshole tried to seal her up. It was full of women.

"Trucks are full of women," I called out quietly over comms so everyone would know to watch their aim. Then, I popped off a round in the man's head who had just closed up the truck. I didn't bother reopening it yet, because the women were safer where they were for now. Instead, I moved to the cab of the truck, and watched as Spike popped a round in the bastard there who had been about to start the truck. I grabbed his gun and ammo, then tucked it away as I kept going.

"Truck two, clear," Wren called out over comms for himself and Stone.

"Truck one, clear," I answered back knowing Spike and I had just taken out the players in the room and truck around us. That meant there were probably four down of the fifteen we were expecting. That was if there hadn't been any others hiding below ground. Clearly, they'd had the women hidden somewhere, so it was possible we would be seeing a whole lot more action.

"Breaching north door," Ghost called out. There was a resounding boom in the air as the explosives they used to blow the door did the job.

"Breaching west door," Battle's voice reverberated through the comms. Battle was one of the men in the Sierra High Chapter. He'd been with them for about eight years now, and was the reason the guys were using strip framed charges that targeted the area better than the way we used to do things. Battle had been demolitions in the military before he was retired early and sought out the comfort of a new band of brothers. Heavy, Shorty, and Six-Pack were with him.

"Breaching South door," Tuck answered back.

"Breaching East," Grim announced a half a second later. When he didn't report casualties, I knew Chief was okay too.

We had Ghost, Sweet, Phoenix, and Hold 'Em on the north door since it was the only exit point on the backside of the building. All other entry points had two men breaching each door or truck bay. That kept us spread out, but able to maintain the exits at the same time.

"Two down on truck 1," I called out.

"Three on north door," Ghost chimed in, followed quickly by Wren. "Two down on truck 2."

"One down on west door, one rabbit headed east," Battle called out.

"Two on south door, we got your rabbit," Tuck answered back.

As we moved further into the building from the loading bays, I noticed movement to my right, between the truck bay I was coming out of and the one I knew Wren and Stone were still in. The man there was headed in, gun drawn before I popped him full of lead and moved the fuck on. "Another down between loading bays," I stated quietly enough that comms picked it up, but my voice didn't carry far. That brought us up to 12 bodies dropped. That meant, if our intel was correct, there should only be three men left.

Wren and Stone pulled up on our rear and started clearing our side toward the south door. Grim and Chief moved toward the north door, clearing shit as they went. Ghost and Sweet split off to the right, heading toward the west door while Hold 'Em and Phoenix moved toward Grim and Chief. Once we all cleared the entire building it quickly became clear that we were still missing a few men who should have been there.

"Someone go open up one of those trucks and let's get those women talking. They had to be storing them somewhere, which means there could still be more men."

"Already on it," Wren answered back.

I moved further out from the middle of the room where we'd all converged after clearing the room, and that's when I finally happened to look up. "Scatter!" I yelled just before a fucking grenade was dropped from the rafters.

I shot the bastard, but it was already too late by then. Luckily, the damn thing rolled just far enough away from where the men had done exactly as I had said and scattered, that I didn't there would be any major injuries on our side. Still, just to be sure that didn't happen again, I scanned the rest of the rafters. There were no more men hiding in them, which meant we still had two bodies unaccounted for, and I didn't like the fact that Ivan Stasevich wasn't among the men we'd already taken out. He was the one who had ordered the hit on an Aces High MC family in order to shake us up and get us to turn over Shep's family.

"The women say there's an access in the men's bathroom to the downstairs level. There's barely any room to stand down there according to what they said. It's more like a root cellar, but a couple of the girls aren't on the trucks that were with them."

"They think the assholes are down there helping themselves to the merchandise?" I asked Wren.

"That's exactly what the women thought. One of them was reportedly a virgin that Stasevich wanted to break in himself. The other was a labeled a mouthy bitch who needed to learn a lesson," Wren repeated what he'd been told.

I was already moving toward the bathroom in question in the northwest corner of the building. "Smoke!" I heard Ghost calling out to me, but I didn't halt my movements. "Smoke! Damn it! Stop. Heavy and Grim could both use some patching up back there."

"I'm not the only one trained in first aid here," I told him as I continued on.

"No, you're not. You're also not the only one who lost someone to these assholes. We need to be able to question Stasevich. There may be more women out there."

"Are you fuckin' kidding me right now?"

"No, I'm not. I need to know you can handle your shit down there. Otherwise, you need to stay up here and patch up your brothers while we get the two assholes who are left."

"I can handle myself," I assured him. I wasn't sure I was being completely honest with Ghost and myself at that point, and judging from the look he threw my way, he wasn't so sure himself. Still, Tuck stayed behind to patch the men up instead.

As soon as we were down in the tunnel, it took an immediate left and led toward a room that was clearly cut out just beneath the center of the building above us. The floors were natural earth, and the walls were as well. At least someone had been smart enough to actually brace the place properly to keep it from caving in on them, though from the looks of it, there was a portion of the carved out hallway that looked as if it had taken some damage from the grenade that went off above us. Loose soil was spattered all around and there was a clear fracture of the wood bracing the ceiling up above us.

"That doesn't look too stable anymore," Battle managed to say what we were all thinking as we warily walked beneath it anyway to get to the other men and women who were hidden away down there.

No sooner did we get within five feet of the mouth of the room before bullets started flying. "Shit!" I heard Shorty call out. "Hit."

"How bad?" I asked.

"Flesh wound," he called back.

"What the fuck you complaining for then?" Phoenix asked. "Start shooting back."

"Hold your fire until you have your target in sight. There are women down here."

I heard Phoenix grumble something and knew that he wasn't the type to care if there were casualties so long as we won the war without any further harm coming to our own men. It was part of the reason he stayed a nomad. He couldn't handle the social norms the rest of us recognized. We didn't kill women and children if it could be helped, and we considered men taking some damage as a result to be acceptable.

Still, we managed to gain entrance to the room. Once we did, the two men standing guard over a woman who was tied to a post in the middle of the room were taken out quickly.

Each was dropped with a shot to the chest. The woman tied to the post was screaming bloody murder while the other was tossed aside on the dirt floor in a corner looking completely broken. She was lying in a pool of what looked to be mud, but I knew it was her blood that had to be mixing with the dirt on the ground around her.

"Jesus," Chief called out as he went to her first. I glanced around noticing a partitioned off portion of the underground area. That was where I found Ivan cowering like the little bitch he was as he attempted to load his revolver quietly.

"A revolver, Ivan? Really?" I asked as I pointed my Springfield XD-S 4.0 right at his temple. Some of the guys laughed at it saying it was too small to do any damage. I'd since proven that to be false. For a little, easily concealed weapon, it managed to pack a hell of a punch. I was all for using Ivan's head to punch a hole through to show the guys just how effective it could be too.

"Smoke!" I heard Ghost and grinned down at Ivan as I tapped the barrel of the gun to his head.

"They want me to keep you breathing. Do you deserve to take another breath, Ivan?"

He spat at my feet in response. I removed the gun from his temple and knelt down so I could be at eye level with the bastard then I grinned at him. "You don't deserve a quick death, fucker." Then I stood and walked away to let Ghost and Sweet handle him.

"How is she?" I asked as I moved quickly back to the woman I'd noticed earlier.

"She ain't good, that's for sure," Six-Pack told me as I

drew closer. He leaned in. "I think it would be a mercy for us to let her die judging by her injuries."

"Was she the mouth or the virgin?" I asked.

"I'm guessing the mouth," he informed me. "That one back there keeps thanking Hold 'Em for saving her virtue."

"Good thing he already has a road name or that shit might need to be changed," I joked.

"No doubt," he explained as he helped me lift the woman.

"We need to get her upstairs before this whole place destabilizes. I don't want to bring the med kit down here." As if to hurry us, we all heard another small rumbling as dirt and debris fall loose from the ceiling where the beams had been cracked by the grenade.

Once we got the woman upstairs, the severity of her wounds became far more apparent. The sheer amount of filth in the wounds was going to make them extremely hard to treat. I suddenly wished Surfer hadn't just had his own issues with another club and a missing kid, because we could have used him here with us.

"Jesus fuck!" Spike hissed as we passed him with the woman.

"Someone call for the prospects to get their asses over here. We're going to need both the vans and maybe one of those trucks too."

"Any clue what we're doing with the women?" Spike asked.

"That's for Sweet and Ghost to decide."

"We're taking them to Angel Girl. The women want to help them out, get information, and get them back to their families if they have them, or keep them on to help rehabilitate them after their ordeal. MiMi started up this thing for victims of sex trafficking," Sweet told us as he moved over to check out the woman we'd brought up. "She going to make it?"

I shrugged my shoulders. "She's a mess. We're going to need to get her clean and then get her some real medical attention."

"No," the woman hissed out. "No help," we all heard her clear as a bell.

"If we don't get you help, you could die," I explained.

"Then let me," she managed to get out before she passed out once more.

"Over my dead fuckin' body," Spike growled.

"Let's get her loaded up in one of the trucks. I'm not putting her in the van with Ivan. He doesn't get to see the condition he left her in."

"Agreed," Ghost called out as he brought Ivan up with his head bagged. The asshole laughed.

"Too late, already know what I did to her body. It used to be lush, now she'll always remember what I did to her. It's written there in blood, skin, and maybe down to the bone." His cackling laughter was cut off by a swift kick to the groin from Spike.

"Oh, sorry, I bet you felt that balls deep, huh asshole?" It was Spike's turn to laugh. "Don't worry, there's more where that came from."

It took another three hours to get everyone out, back to the barn where we'd stored our bikes, and we did what we could to render the old factory to dust and ash. All the bodies were put down in the underground area and they were doused and set fire to first. Then, the upstairs was doused and burned too. Everything had to go. We weren't stupid. They'd eventually find the bodies, but we knew how to make sure they were never linked to our club.

Once we got back I took the injured woman into the farm house to get her cleaned up. Journey, the woman who was once a member of the S.H.E. MC helped me to clean the wounds so that we wouldn't have to invite more men in than myself to take care of the woman. I was already dreading her waking up and freaking out about me being there with her unclothed body.

Hell, the woman was a complete wreck. Her torso had been carved up with 'Ivan's Whore'. 'Mouthy Bitch' had been carved into her upper back above her shoulder blades, and шлюха was carved into her lower back like a tramp stamp. "What does it mean?" Journey asked me.

I looked it up using my cell. "Whore," I told her.

"Those fuckers," she hissed out. "You know the girls are going to be all over this trying to find out who the bastards were selling the girls to."

"I get it. I'm sure our clubs will be working together on that front."

Journey shook her head. "I can't believe this is still such a prevalent thing. You would think we had already cut the head off this particular dragon before, but it just comes back with more heads each time."

"You take out the leaders and it creates a vacuum that needs to be filled," I explained to her. "When one organization drops the torch, another will gladly pick it up. There are too many depraved assholes in this world willing to pay to ruin people's lives for this to ever come to an end."

"That's part of the reason I had to get away for a while. I love her for doing it, but MiMi kept dragging more sad-sack cases into the club, and I just couldn't handle hearing another story like theirs. I needed a break."

"I get that. Just remember, for every sad story you heard, there's another person who was saved and is able to heal now."

I stayed and watched out for the woman to make sure she was healing okay and that the antibiotics we were able to give her were going to help stave off the worst of it. She seemed to be doing well, considering her wounds. It had been 12 hours since we liberated the women from the factory. It was high time I found where and what they were doing with Ivan, and I had a feeling that would be happening in the barn.

"Where is everyone?"

"There's a small shed out in the woods about fifty yards in," Sweet told me.

"He still alive?"

"For now."

I tipped my head up at Sweet and then moved out there to see for myself. "He give anything up yet?"

"From what I hear he's been pissing himself to tattle on everyone all morning. Was sealed up tighter than Fort Knox until Spike took a run at him."

"Damn." I wondered about the man's motivation because he seemed pretty shook up about the fact that the woman we'd rescued had been so abused.

"He had a woman once, lost her to this same shit."

"She was killed?"

"No, only wished she had been."

"She okay now?"

"She is, but it wasn't Spike that got her there, and he still hasn't been able to forgive himself for that."

I didn't bother asking any further questions. It wasn't my business and it wasn't Sweet's story to tell. Instead, I moved on toward the tree line where he indicated I might find the little shed that housed the man responsible for killing my sister and brother-in-law. "He still alive?" I asked Wren, who was standing outside the building keeping guard.

"He is, but he ain't in the best of shape anymore."

"Doesn't deserve to be. Mind if I get in there, or are you under orders to keep me out?"

"Wouldn't keep you out even if I had been ordered. You do what you need to for Soph, and we'll figure the rest out another way if we need to," he told me. I patted his shoulder and then opened the barn door. The stench hit me immediately. Hot piss, coppery blood, and on top of that was that acrid smell of shit. Since I didn't see a bucket anywhere for the man to relieve himself I figured he had shit himself at some point.

"Well, Ivan, if my nose doesn't deceive me I'd say you smell worse than a preschool full of kids who failed potty training." The man said nothing, simply grunted a response. I turned to Ghost, "You get anything from him?"

"We got plenty," he indicated with his head that I could take my turn now, but before I could get even a swing in, Ghost stopped me when his cell started ringing.

"Give me a minute. I want to be here for this." Ghost stepped out then and took only a few minutes before he poked his head back in and called me out.

"What's up?" I asked as I moved out of the building and shut the wooden door behind me. Ghost did not look pleased.

"There's a situation at home," he explained.

"What kind of situation?"

"It's Poppy. Leanne has Brant and Bubba with her, but they found Poppy unconscious at the house. She was really sick, and they're not sure if the fever took her down or if she knocked her head when she fell."

"What the fuck?" I yelled.

"Where is she now?"

"She's at the hospital getting looked at. Leanne says she's not doing well, still hasn't woken up yet." I stood there, momentarily stunned by the news.

"The baby?"

"Don't know anything else yet." He glanced behind me at the shed. "We can try to keep him alive for you, but..."

"I don't give a fuck about that. End him. I need to get to Poppy and Brant. Poor little man must be scared out of his mind."

I already showed Journey what to do for the chick we found. Make sure she gets that medication, or whoever takes her knows how to dose her properly and for how long. It's really important considering the condition we found her in."

"I got it. We'll make sure everything is taken care of. Update me as soon as you know anything," Ghost told me, as if his wife wouldn't be doing that already.

I knew why he insisted on it though. He wanted to make sure I was alright while we waited to see how Poppy pulled through. Hell, I was already beating myself up over the fact that I didn't even know she was sick once again. Never again. This kind of thing would never happen with us again. From here on out, Poppy and me were going to be partners in every way, and that included letting each other know if we so much as got the fucking sniffles.

17. AT YOUR FEET

SHE LOOKED SO SMALL LYING THERE IN THE BED WITH THE WHITE hospital blanket pulled up to her breasts and her hair slicked back on her forehead by sweat from the fever she'd had. My chest ached as I took it all in. Poppy had never once, in the time I'd known her, appeared weak. That was what hurt the most. I left her to end up in this situation while I was chasing vengeance. I knew I needed to do it in order to keep her safe too, but at what consequence? We almost lost her anyway.

"She'll be okay," a man called out from the dark corner of the room where he was propped in a chair with his feet resting on a little table he'd pulled around.

"What the fuck are you doing here?"

"Didn't anyone tell you?" he asked, a certain amount of smugness present in his voice. I just stood there and stared at him. "I'm the one that found her."

"I thought Leanne found her," I said.

"No, Leanne came not too long after I arrived, but when I

saw they were in trouble I called for help. The kid was screaming his head off, the dog looked antsy as fuck."

"Bubba didn't attempt to attack you?"

"No. Leanne showed up, and had a key to get in and got a hold of Bubba first. Apparently, Poppy had texted her and told her she wasn't feeling well." Snake stated coolly.

"Why weren't you with the men in Goldsboro?"

"I had already been on my way here to see Poppy when the call went out. I was too far out. They said they'd roll without me." He shrugged his shoulders.

"What were you doing coming to see her anyway?"

"We're friends. No matter what."

"Such good friends you never bothered to give her a head's up that her man was cheating on her for years? You had to know."

"I knew. I hinted around to her for years, but she never got it."

"Why not come out and say it?"

He huffed. "Walker's my club brother. I couldn't come out and tell her. You know how it is."

I gave him a scathing look. "I think an exception would have been made considering her brother is also in the club and would want her protected."

He scoffed. "You know shit don't work that way. She chose to land herself with a brother, for better or worse."

"I think you had another reason for not wanting to be the one to tell her."

"Yeah, I did." His admission came with a bit of aggression in his voice. "I wanted her for myself, and I knew she would never come to me if I was the one who told her."

"She would never come to you after, because you weren't the one man enough to tell her in the beginning though," I insisted.

"Yeah, didn't see that one coming, I'll be honest." He scuffed a foot across the floor as he stood and moved deeper into the shadows. "I was going to transfer up here when I realized she was moving. I talked to Sweet about it, and he saw right through my reasons."

"He wouldn't let you?" I asked, actually surprised.

"No, he fuckin' wouldn't. Said he'd get Ghost to block the transfer himself if he had to. Poppy deserved a clean break from the boys of Sierra High is what he told me."

"Can't say he was wrong there either."

"Then she met you," he spat out.

"Do you think if there was any part of her pining away for you that she would have made that instant connection with me the way she did?"

Snake huffed and ran his hand across the clean shaven side of his head. Both sides had been shaved down leaving only a short mohawk down the middle. "Walk came back fucked up after he was up here last. We all thought he had been in Florida visiting family. That's where he told Sweet he was headed. Only thing I got out of him, when he was barely conscious, was that Poppy got everything she ever wanted and it wasn't with him."

"You needed to see for yourself?"

"Yeah, I did." He turned and looked me right in the eye then. "I fucked up with her all those years ago. I wanted her from the moment I saw her, only I was distracted that night and Walk got to her first. Knew from first sight she was going to be a special kind of woman. I should have fought for her then before he got his hooks into her. Hell, we all knew that dick would never be any good to a woman." He shook his head and then let it hang there on his shoulders a minute before meeting my eyes again. "You take better care of her, you hear me?"

"I hear you," I promised him. "I know it's little consolation when your feelings are involved, but I love her. She's every damn thing to me."

"Good. Make sure you show her that every fuckin' day, because Walk sure as fuck didn't. Now, he's drowning himself in rotgut liquor to try to forget how bad he fucked it all up."

"You heading back to Georgia?"

"Nah. I'm gonna stick around until she comes back to the land of the living. Came to see my girl, gonna make sure she knows I was here."

"She ain't your girl," I insisted.

"She'll always be my girl. It's just in different way than I'd hoped she would be." I nodded my head at the man. I couldn't begrudge him having a part in her life. He may not have been upfront with her about what a club brother was doing behind her back, but he still managed to be the only one of those fuckers down there who cared enough to see that she was doing okay.

I moved away from him and dragged the other chair to sit beside her. Her hand was cold when I picked it up and put it in my own. "I'll give you my warmth, baby. You take it, my strength, and anything else you need from me to get better, honey. I need you. We took care of business and everything is going to be just fine now. There's no more danger waiting on the horizon. That means we have more family days like the one we had before I went to work. Remember Brant's face when he saw that blanket fort in the backyard? He lit up like fireworks on the Fourth of July. I can't wait to be sitting out there with you guys while watching you nurse our baby too." I let my other hand slide down her blanket covered body until it rested over her belly. I need you to get better for the baby too. You still have a long way to go, honey.

"That's all she ever wanted," Snake spoke up, nodding towards where my hand was. "She wanted a baby so bad, and every time I saw Walker running off with another woman I just wanted to put him to ground myself. Don't know why he was so fuckin' stupid that he couldn't see a good woman when she was right in front of him."

"Don't know, but I'm thankful for it."

"Yeah, I guess you are. I'm heading downstairs to grab some coffee. Need me to get you anything?"

I shook my head. "Got everything I need right here," I answered.

I could have sworn I heard him mumble, "Lucky fucker," before he left the room, but I didn't disagree so I didn't bother to verify either. Instead I just sat there and tried to channel my strength into my woman. Then I got an idea and reached into my pocket for my cell phone.

"I need a favor from Leanne," I told Ghost.

"What kind of favor?" he asked.

Then I told him my plan. In the end he just chuckled. "Guess we all should have seen this coming. You do realize she ain't exactly in a position to make anything official yet, right?"

"She will be though, and until she is, I want every fucker out there to know she's taken. More importantly, I want her to know that she is."

"Don't worry, we'll make it happen, brother. Any updates yet?"

"No changes. She's still in and out of it from what I've seen since I've been here."

"Was Snake there?"

"Still is, just went for some coffee."

"That going okay?"

I sighed. "I'm sure it isn't easy for him, but he understands the score anyway."

"Good, been worried about that one. He went above Sweet, asked for a transfer after she got here. I told him to give her a year, because there was no way she'd be receptive to him, since he was Walker's best friend there. I knew it would take a little time to put the worst of her memories behind her." It was Ghost's turn to sigh. "Some things were never meant to be. I figure, if it had been meant to be, years wouldn't have been wasted with him watching his buddy fuck her over."

"Can't say I'm sad about it," I told him and Ghost laughed.

"No, I guess you aren't. You take care of that girl, you hear me? She's a special one. They don't come around all that often, not for men like us."

"Seems you got lucky twice."

"Yeah, I did, because I'm an incredibly lucky fucker. Don't

think you're gonna be me though, so you better hang on tight to what you got and never forget how precious it is." With that, he hung up.

"I know exactly what I've got, don't I, honey?" I asked my still sleeping Poppy. Sitting here with her looking so fucking small and exhausted took something from me. I never wanted to see my woman looking so helpless again. If I could help it, I would make sure nothing like this ever happened again. I should have been home with her. Hell, I should have at least left someone there with her. Something.

"No time for regrets," a familiar voice called out from the door before he came closer and offered me a cup of coffee I had declined earlier.

"Not regrets so much as learning lessons. She won't be left on her own from now on if I have to leave on club business."

Snake chuckled. "If you think Poppy will take well to having a babysitter, then you haven't really gotten to know her well at all."

"I know she wouldn't want a fuckin' babysitter. That doesn't mean some old ladies won't stop by and keep her company, help out with getting her business off the ground up here, and whatever else she might need, especially since she's pregnant and has my nephew to care for when I'm not around. It's a lot to take on for one person without help."

"Well, might not want to let on that the old ladies are following your orders to stop in then."

I turned narrowed eyes on him. "Unlike in that shit hole, backwoods town you live in, the women here love Poppy. I wouldn't have to order them to do shit."

To my surprise, Snake nodded his head. "Good. I hated it for her that she felt so abandoned by everyone when everything went down." He sighed. "Of course, I knew then that she'd never stick around. She's not one to suffer fake people in her life once she realizes they haven't been genuine."

"That why you asked to transfer? You knew she'd never come back there?"

"She's the reason. The only reason."

"I want to feel bad for you, but I don't." The admission rolled off my tongue before I could pull it back. Snake just laughed.

"Don't pity me, asshole. I'm the king of bad fucking timing, or luck, or whatever the fuck. Still, I wouldn't trade her friendship for anything. She's one of the most decent people I've ever met in this life. If it couldn't be me, looks like she didn't do too bad with you."

I wanted to punch him in the face on some level, but I also knew exactly where he was coming from. Before anything more could be said, the door to the room opened and Ghost, Leanne and Brantley came in. Brant looked almost scared as he scanned the room until his eyes landed on me.

"Hey little man," I called out softly, and he came barreling for me. I snatched him up into the air and then pulled him close for a hug.

"Is Popwee otay?"

"She's just resting, buddy. Poppy was pretty sick."

He stuck his bottom lip out. "She needed hews mommy to gets hew betta?"

"Poppy's mommy is in heaven with yours, little man. She

just needed to see the doctor for some medicine to help get her better. She's going to be fine okay?"

"Otay." I turned to look back at the woman in question, who appeared to be sleeping peacefully now. Brant tugged on my shirt. "I wuv Popwee," he whispered against my chest.

"Me too, little man. Me too."

At that moment, I was a bit surprised by the person who came through the door. He cleared his throat before walking over to where I sat next to Poppy with Brant on my lap. He bent down beside me, talking low as he did. "I came to see if you needed any help. I didn't realize Poppy was sick or that she was the one taking care of Brant all this time," he told me, though there was no accusation in his tone.

"Someone had to do it, and I work too," I explained.

Kent shook his head. "No, I know that. I just took for granted that the same people I was blaming for our sister's death would step up and care for little man there when I wasn't doing it myself." He offered a humorless chuckle as he said the words. "I'm sorry, Smoke. I know how much they all loved her and Bender. It wasn't fair to put that on everyone."

"No, it wasn't," I confirmed. "But they all understood anyway," I told him as I tilted my head in Poppy's direction. "Especially her."

"She's a keeper," he told me.

"I know it."

"Would you mind if I took Brant and spent some time with him today? Maybe we could hang out at your apartment?" Kent asked me.

"How about I give you the keys to Poppy's place and you take him there and check in on Bubba for us too?"

"You got it. Smoke, I really am sorry," he offered.

"No need, little brother. I understand too. It's okay."

"It's not okay, but I will make it up to you."

Kent had only been gone a few minutes after leaving with Brantley, when Leanne approached me. "Here's what you asked for. I got Surfer to find it in your apartment rather than going there myself," Leanne explained as she put the little white box in my hand. "How long have you had it?"

I smirked at her, because I knew she was wondering when I'd possibly had a chance to go get an engagement ring for Poppy. "I've had it for a while now," I told her, and it was true. The ring had come to me when my mother died. It had belonged to her mother. My grandparents had died together when I was little, but my mom used to always tell me the story of their love. She said it was a thing of beauty, something meant to last beyond this lifetime and right into the next. Before she died, she put this box in my hands and told me that the woman who would wear it one day would make it obvious immediately that she was meant for it. Julie never had. I knew she would never wear it. The first time I went home after meeting Poppy, I went in search of the ring.

I opened the box, knowing that the room had filled up with more people who had come to wish Poppy well, but not caring that they were all there. I took the ring out of the box and glanced down at it. I'd asked my mother once why the ring had never come to her, and she told me she had a shot at the kind of happiness that ring symbolized, and she gave it up for the wrong man – my father. She told me she'd never regret her choice because it left her with her three loves, but that the ring was never meant for her.

I took Poppy's hand and slid it on her finger. "You were meant to be mine, Poppy. I knew it from the minute we first met. Everything I'd ever questioned in this life just suddenly clicked into place when I looked into your beautiful green eyes, honey. There was no going back after that. Not for me, and not for you either, because I know you felt it too. I'm not some dumb boy. I'm claiming what's mine, and I'll be there to take care of you and all of our children from now until we no longer walk this earth. I'll be there in the next life too, waiting for you to find me. That's how sure I am."

I took the other thing that Leanne had brought for me. My acoustic guitar, a Fender Dreadnought, and started playing one of her favorite songs. I figured if my sort of demanding proposal didn't wake her, maybe a little music would. I played quietly for a few minutes before the spell was broken. Someone must have accidentally hit the remote control because the television in the room suddenly turned on glaringly loud. "No," I heard Poppy mumble.

She was coming around, and I wasn't done talking, despite the noise and shuffling from the people in the room trying to shut the tv off again. I set the guitar to the side and laid my head down next to her own. "As soon as you're better, we'll work out a date to go get it done. I'm not waiting anymore on what everyone else thinks is appropriate. Screw them! I already know everything I need to. You're my woman, you're carrying my baby, and we're already a family so nothing else matters. We'll just be making it official." I kissed her on the cheek and laid my head down beside hers again, watching her as she fought to wake up. Hell, maybe she was fighting to stay asleep. All I knew was that she was gorgeous lying there in that bed. I brushed some hair out of her face and smiled at her as her eyes opened and her lips tipped up at the sight of me. Someone across the room moved, scraping the chair against the floor and destroying our moment. I wanted to roar and pounce on every last asshole in the room and kick them all out, but I couldn't move away from her.

She took in all the faces of the people who loved her and had been worried for her. Then she reached up to run her hand through her hair, only she managed to snag some of it on the ring I'd put on her finger. I gently reached out and grabbed her hand to keep her from pulling harder and ripping at her hair. I took a moment to untangle her hair from the ring facets and then I watched as her eyes lighted on the sparkle coming off of the diamond in the center of the ring. Then she took a look around at everyone to see who was in on it, and then back to me. I couldn't fathom what she was thinking in that moment, but instead of asking about the ring she glanced around the room once more and asked after my nephew instead. "Brant?"

The pallor of her face changed as the blood drained out of it and I watched panic take over. The machine attached to her started going a little nuts as her heart rate increased.

"Shh, calm down, honey. He's fine." I soothed, though the words didn't seem to penetrate whatever state she was in. "He's okay. He's with Kent right now. He's taking care of Bubba too, honey. They're both fine. Leanne got there not long after your text."

"The baby?" Her next question shouldn't have surprised

me. She was worried about everyone else first. Typical Poppy.

"Just fine. They brought an ultrasound in, and we all got to see the heart beat and everything."

"How long have I been here?" I heard the light strings of my guitar being strummed by someone, but I didn't bother to see who had picked it up as I answered Poppy.

"Two days. Leanne was here with you until we got back. Everyone just stopped in to check on you at the perfect time though since you finally decided to stay awake."

"I'm so sorry," she told me as tears began to form.

"You couldn't help getting sick," I admonished her.

"But Brant-"

"Stop! You let Leanne know something was wrong, and you did your best. Nobody is blaming you for anything. Brant was obviously worried about you, but he was fine. He just sat there with you until Leanne got there. He wasn't harmed, and it's not like you neglected him. You got sick and passed out. That is more my fault for leaving you with him so long with no help."

"Enough of that shit from both of you," Chief called out as he put my guitar back down. "Neither of you are at fault. It is what it is. Shit happens, and then we get over it and move on. I'm glad you're getting better, Sis. You had us all worried! Don't ever do it again though!" Chief moved to the opposite side of the bed that I was on and leaned in to give his sister a kiss on the forehead before he scrunched up his face and pulled away. "Maybe you should try to get up and get a shower sometime soon though, you stink!" Poppy playfully swatted at her brother, but I could see that even doing that much took it out of her, so I stood and turned to look at everyone who was still gathered in the room.

"Chief is right, Poppy stinks!" Everyone laughed as Poppy attempted to hide her embarrassment underneath a pillow. "I think maybe you should give us some time to get her cleaned up and back home, and then you can all stop in see her."

"Don't listen to these brutes, sweetie! You look fabulous, even in your sweat-soaked state. I'll be around to check in on you as soon as you're back home, okay?" Leanne asked, finally coaxing Poppy back out from underneath her pillow. "I'm really happy to see you're feeling better. You scared the daylights out of me when I showed up and saw Snake was pounding on the door."

"Snake?" Poppy asked. "What do you mean Snake was pounding on the door?

Snake managed to pop back in the room as if he had been summoned. "Ah, she's finally awake, I see." He wasted no time replacing Chief's place on the opposite side of the bed from me. I didn't miss the lingering glance he gave to the ring that now sat on her finger. Not that I wanted to be that dick, but it pleased me a bit to see the pain in his eyes when he saw it. I needed him to know, in no uncertain terms, that she was mine. Now and forever. That quick flash of pain didn't stop the bastard from leaning over and kissing my woman's face though. I growled low in my throat, a warning to the fucker that he was treading on awful thin ice.

"Hey, sweet girl, how you feeling?" He gave her a small

smile as she looked between the two of us. "I see you didn't waste time moving on from Walker." Poppy did not look happy at his announcement, but before she could rip him a new one, he threw his hands up in surrender. "I'm not judging, you know that. I just didn't realize you had gotten so serious so fast."

"Didn't Walk tell you about his trip here last week?"

Snake shifted uncomfortably then. "He mentioned seeing you, but didn't go into too much detail." He turned to me then.

I nodded my head acknowledging the fact that we hadn't actually talked about Walker's visit earlier when it was mentioned. "He confronted Poppy before I could make it there. Seemed pretty sure of himself that he was going to sweep in, apologize, and carry her home with him on the back of his bike."

Snake laughed. "No wonder he came back from his trip and sank into the bottom of a bottle."

"You knew about his trip, and no one sent a heads up?" I groused.

"Nah, like I said earlier, we knew he was going on a trip, only he was supposed to be headed south to see family in Tallahassee. Thought maybe his ma took a turn for the worse when he showed up drowning his sorrows." Shit, he had told me that. Having my woman lying in a hospital bed was fucking with my mind.

"Is she not doing well?" Poppy asked, seeming genuinely concerned, and pulling me from my own thoughts.

"Cancer's back from what I hear. Though, I don't hear

much from him directly these days since he seems to think he picked sides between you and him."

"I'm sorry," Poppy started to apologize.

Snake simply waved her off. "Nah, don't you go worrying about that. I just did the right thing when he wouldn't, and he's mad about that. One day he'll realize he's mad at himself and not me."

"You came to my house and found me?" she asked, changing the subject.

"I did. I wasn't sure what kind of support system you had up here, and after I found out about Walker's visit, I figured you could use a friendly face." Snake glanced over at me and I just tipped my head the slightest bit to indicate I'd go along with what he was saying. He had come for her, not to check on her. She didn't need to know that though. "No one answered the door even though I could hear the dog barking and a kid crying inside," he told her. I wished he had left the last part out. She didn't need to feel any more guilt over passing out in front of Brant. "I took a look in the window and saw you on the floor." He put a hand over his chest rubbed where his heart was. "Took at least a year off my life to see that."

I couldn't help that growl that his admission brought out of me again. This fucker was starting to get under my skin, and he knew it. "I know she's your woman, I got that. She's been my friend for a long damn time now though, so calm down with that growling bullshit. I'm not a threat. She's never looked at me the way she does you. There's not a damn thing for you to worry over."

Poppy snickered and then it turned into a full-blown laugh as she took in the jealousy written all over my face. That was when I knew I had to leave and give them some time to talk without my being there. She was mine. I knew she was. That didn't mean I could stand to watch a man who had been pining over her for years talk to her with a familiarity that, in some ways, we were still working on together. "I'm going to grab a coffee then find the nurse to hunt down the doctor to see when we can spring you from this joint. You two catch up until then."

Ghost and Chief followed me out of the room, and we all made our way to the end of the hallway. "You doing okay?" Chief asked.

"As good as I can considering my woman's sitting in a hospital bed because she was so sick that she passed out and stayed asleep for two fucking days."

Ghost clutched onto my shoulder. "You have a strong woman there. It'll all work out."

"Speaking of working out," I started to say, and then I launched into my plan to buy a house big enough to accommodate our growing family. "I need you both to be on the lookout for something with enough room, and in a nice school district, but close to the club."

"Jesus, you already sound like Mr. Mom," Chief teased.

"Don't laugh, Chief. You'll find yourself settling down soon enough."

Chief scoffed and then the two of them bantered back and forth as I got lost in my head with my own plans for the future. Of course, I never saw a trip to Georgia in our plans, but that's exactly what happened. We ended up heading down there for a court ordered mediation where upon seeing my, by then, very pregnant fiancé, the court finally granted Poppy her divorce. Though, it didn't turn out all roses seeing as to how we ended up in the damn hospital one more time for our troubles.

18. BABY GIRL

Sweat dripped from her hairline as she grimaced while clutching her belly again. I knew this trip to Georgia was going to be fucked from the beginning since we had to deal with Walker trying once again, to hang on to the scraps of what he thought he had left with Poppy. It didn't work. What it did do was add stress to my woman that sent her into labor early.

"Ow! It fucking hurts!"

"I can tell, honey." Just watching her go through this shit was painful for me. I couldn't imagine actually having to live through it. I had wanted a big family with Poppy, but I was beginning to rethink things when she asked me a stupid fucking question that caught me off guard for a just a moment.

"How can you tell?"

"You mean besides the fact that you're dropping f-bombs left and right and damn near ripping my arm off with each..." I stopped speaking dead in my tracks as she gripped on to me with claws from hell and refused to let go. The pinch and scalding hot sting as two of them pierced my skin didn't even phase me beyond the initial reaction my body had to the onslaught of pain.

"Damn, dude, that looks like it hurts," I heard Chief interject into the situation.

"Why is he still here?" Poppy cried out while trying to see around me to find her brother, as if he could possibly be just a disembodied voice in the room.

"I was just dropping off your bag since you two were out of the house so fast you forgot it."

"Hi, everyone! How is our patient doing today?" A nurse who looked as though she should still be in high school asked in a chipper manner as she skipped her ass into the room. She was wearing scrubs, but the damn things were so tight they were highlighting every damn curve she had. Something I was sure Chief had noticed, and appreciated, considering how his tongue was still wagging in her direction.

"I'm doing," Poppy started to answer before another contraction rolled through her. If her reaction was anything to gauge it by, this one was the mother of all fucking contractions, because I kid you not, she was about to start speaking in tongues. At least that was what I thought before she opened her mouth and started yelling at the too-perky-for-her-own-good nurse. "FUCK THIS SHIT, I'm not doing just fine at all! Get this baby out of me!"

"Oh dear, that sounds like it was a bad one." The nurse was clearly an idiot for speaking to a woman in pain like that. Poppy looked fit to be tied, and damn near reared up off the bed. I stepped a little closer to hold her down if I needed to, because I couldn't allow her to go off and start a fucking brawl with the nurse while she was in active labor with our child.

"Honey, you're doing just fine. You use as many f-bombs as you need. I'm sure they won't be our child's first word," I told her. Okay, now I was the one poking fun at her because she had told me that I wasn't allowed to curse once she went into labor because she didn't want the baby's first words she heard being an f-bomb.

"Oh, God, something's happening down there," Poppy hissed out and I nearly made the mistake of looking. Only Chief's vehement shaking of his head caught my attention first and managed to warn me away from looking.

The nurse proved herself to be the idiot I thought she was. "It's a bit too early for all that. I'll be checking you in just a few minutes when the doctor comes in. She glanced down at the little tablet in her hand and nodded her head as if she needed to agree with herself. "Yep, it says here that your nurse prior to shift change just checked you about forty-five minutes ago."

"There is a head coming out of my body, and it burns like a motherfucker!" Poppy seethed at the woman.

That was the moment I lost my damn mind and moved just enough so that I could take a look between Poppy's spread legs. A knee to the face stopped me from actually seeing anything this time! I had to physically shake the blow off, and apparently it did not knock any fucking sense into me whatsoever because I kept on moving around the offending leg and managed to see what my woman had been screaming about. Sure as fuck, there was a head full of hair staring at me from between Poppy's legs. "There's a head, get the goddamn doctor in here, now!"

Bubbles, what I had dubbed the dumb bitch of a nurse in my head, jumped into action and ran to the bottom of the bed, dropping the end portion out from under Poppy's feet. The nurse caught one of her calves in her hand, and I instinctively managed to grab the other which effectively held her splayed out for anyone and everyone in the room to see what was going on down there.

"Shit! I did not need to see that!" Chief yelled just before I noticed him hightail it out of the room. I could hear his loud-mouth at least calling for help as he went though. "I just saw the head, someone better get my sister's doctor in there now!"

"Oh-dear-lord-sweet-baby-jesus-take-the-wheel!" Poppy screamed the last as I watched her push despite the nurse yelling for her not to do it.

"Please, you have to stop pushing, because the doctor isn't here yet."

A doctor came rushing in the room immediately and damn near dove between my woman's legs. Any other time and I might have punched a mother fucker out, but it just so happened that Chief pulled me from my murderous thoughts with his loud as fuck question from the hallway. "Anyone have some whiskey? Jesus, I can't un-see that shit."

"Are you fucking insane?" Poppy screamed at Nurse Bubbles. "Get out! Get the hell out of here. My husband can deliver our baby, because it isn't waiting!"

"Whoa, now, honey. We'll get you there. If you need to push, you push."

The doctor basically shoulder-checked the nurse to push her out of the way. "Get her out!" Poppy yelled some more.

After Bubbles gave a feeble attempt at protesting the order, the doctor turned a hell of a glare on her. "You heard the patient. Send someone else in, right now."

"One more good push, and we'll be handing your baby over to you, Poppy!" The doctor explained while the nurse was retreating from the room in tears. I pushed against Poppy's leg to help her as she attempted another push, and then I watched as the relief flooded through her. The tension in her face slackened and she took a deep breath before laying back. That's when I realized it was done and looked back toward the doctor who was now holding a squirming, somewhat bloody body with white shit coating it in spots. The doctor wasted no time in getting rid of his burden on my woman's chest. A new nurse, an older woman, had entered the room and moved quickly with a suction bulb thing to try to clear everything for the baby and then after a few quick seconds, a squall filled up the room as our baby let us know she'd made her entrance into the world and she might not be entirely happy with how that happened.

"It's a girl!" The doctor called out a bit late.

I couldn't take my eyes off of the sight of my daughter lying there on Poppy's chest. They were beautiful. Our daughter was perfect, and my woman was an amazing crea-ture who had just worked her ass off to bring her into this world. I'd never in my life been prouder and more over-whelmed with emotion. No one ever tells you that it's the happiest moment of your life when you get bowled over completely by emotion.

"A baby girl," I finally managed to get out and watched as my baby girl tried to wiggle toward my voice, obviously recognizing the sound.

"You want to do the honors and cut the cord?" The doctor asked me, pulling me out of my reverence. I shook my head indicating that I did not. I tucked a single finger in my daughter's grasp and stood in awe as she clamped her tiny little fingers around my larger one.

"Do you have a name for her?" The nurse asked.

"Sophie," I told her, while trying to get the words past all the emotion that was clogging me throat.

"Layla," Poppy added.

"Lewis," I tacked on in the end while smiling down at Poppy and still holding on to our daughter.

"Sophie Layla Lewis?" The nurse confirmed the name, and we both agreed while watching our daughter. "That's a beautiful name." The nurse did whatever she was doing off to the side before moving back over to the opposite side of the bed than I was on. "I need to get this little one cleaned up for you real quick. I promise I'll bring her back quickly."

I immediately went on edge as I watched Poppy's demeanor change immediately. She didn't want anyone taking her daughter from her, and I couldn't blame her. I wasn't too fond of the idea either. Not even realizing I was doing it, my chest puffed up and I prepared for a fight.

"Calm down, daddy. You can come and watch her get her first bath. She never has to leave your sight." I wanted that, because we were all our daughter had back here to protect her, but at the same time there was no one else here with Poppy aside from the doctor and another nurse who had come in at some point. Still, they were strangers.

"I'd rather you stay with her," Poppy finally said after registering the conflict she could see playing out on my face. I finally agreed and followed the nurse out in the hall. Chief was standing out in the hallway still and when I realized I tipped my head in the direction of the room.

"Stay with her while I go keep an eye on the baby, yeah?"

"Never had to ask, brother. I've got your girl. Go take care of the little one." Chief wasted no time moving back into the room.

I nodded and followed the nurse out of the room, reluctantly leaving behind my love to chase my daughter. Somehow, I felt like this was a bit of foreshadowing. A girl. I was happier than hell to heave a healthy baby girl, but flashes of her teen years starting hitting me as I watched the nurse roughly washing the white cheesy shit and blood from her tiny little body.

"Hey, you need to tone that shit down!" I called to her as the bitch rolled her eyes at me. Did she know who she was fucking with right now?

"Calm down, Mr. Lewis. All babies get this treatment. They're not as breakable as you think, and we need to get her clean."

"So you say," I told her as I glared while she continued to do her thing. My baby girl wasn't even putting up a fuss at all the attention, so I figured all was well.

"Look at this sweet thing. She wants to be clean, don't you, sugar?"

I had to laugh at that. "Don't you laugh, daddy. I betcha any amount of money this little one is going to be the high maintenance type. She gets dirty, it's going to be a screaming fit until she's cleaned up again. Isn't that right, little miss?"

Another nurse came by and tucked a little notecard looking thing into a holder on the back of the plastic bassinet on wheels that had been set aside for my daughter. The card proudly announced that she was Sophie Layla Lewis. The grin on my face at seeing the name Poppy had given her couldn't be contained. Our baby girl had been named after both of our sisters. Baby girl's aunts would never get to know her, but she would carry their memories with her forever.

"Whoa, whoa, what the hell is that?" A second nurse had just approached my daughter with what looked like a security device stores used to put on clothing back in the day. Both nurses smiled at me.

"It's a security device. You and your wife will be given a matching wristband. If anyone other than the two of you attempt to leave the premises with the baby and they don't have the matching band, they will be stopped. If the baby is moved to a location not authorized while wearing the band, it triggers a lockdown of doors and elevators as necessary. Alarms will be triggered if the band is tampered with as well."

"Damn, girl, they knew they had a biker baby coming in and they slapped an ankle monitor on you already. See that, you're already trouble." Both nurses laughed as I continued just watching my daughter, in total awe of her.

"Mr. Lewis, if I could have your left wrist?"

"Sure," I held out my hand to her and she attached a

band to it. I read the information on my band and compared it with what was on Sophie's band. They were a perfect match. "Are we good now? Can we get her back to her momma?"

The older nurse gave the younger one a knowing look. "She's probably tuckered out and sleepin' right now. Why don't you give her a little more time?"

"No offense, lady, but you don't know my woman. She won't rest until her daughter is back in her sight."

"We hear that all the time," the younger nurse tittered just as an intercom went off.

"Is baby girl Lewis ready? Her mother is throwing a fit that her baby hasn't been brought back to her yet."

I just cocked my brow at the two women as if to ask them what they thought now. "Just point the way, ladies," I told them as I took my daughter into my arms.

"Sir, you have to transfer her down the hall while in the bassinet."

I glared at the woman. "If you think you can tell me I can't hold my daughter, you have another thing coming to you, lady."

"Sir, it is hospital policy."

"Well, it's my personal policy to bond with my daughter as much as possible, and that requires actually holding her instead of wheeling her around in a plastic tub." One of those twats could follow me to my woman's room with the fucking tub that my daughter wouldn't be rolling around in as long as I was there.

The minute I walked into the room holding our daughter, Poppy's eyes were all for the baby in my arms. Her smile was something I wish I had been able to take a picture of, because there had never been anything more beautiful on this earth.

"I got it," Chief called out from somewhere to my right.

"Got what?"

"The picture of her face," he told me, and then I turned my gaze from the love of my life to her brother, my club brother, who understood what that moment meant to me. I tipped my chin at him and then went to place our daughter in Poppy's arms.

"She's so sweet, just look at those pouty little lips. Oh my God, she's going to be gorgeous," she cooed at the little bundle.

"Might want to bump up the armory in a few years," I commented. Chief stood and came over to the side of the bed and took a look at his niece.

"I'll help with that."

19. THE HOUSE

Truth be told, I thought I'd have us in a bigger house before the baby came along. There always seemed to be something that got in the way when I thought about house hunting though. Then, our little Sophie-bug came early and well, that meant I had to get creative in order to surprise Poppy. I managed to find one just before we headed down to Georgia, and I put an offer in, but I hadn't heard anything until the day we got back. As much as I didn't want to leave her to her own devices after just giving birth and having to travel with a newborn right after going through that bullshit divorce proceedings, I needed to get help to distract her.

That was where Leanne came in. She managed to weasel her way in the door and asked politely if I wouldn't mind going to help Ghost with some shit they were working on at the club-house. I saw Poppy's eyes dim a bit when I readily agreed. "I'm a phone call away, honey. You need me, I'll come running."

"I need you," she whined.

I smiled down at her as Leanne laughed softly. "Let's have some girl time for a bit and let Smoke go do the guy thing. He'll be back as quickly as he can be."

It took a little more convincing before I managed to make it out the door and down to the real estate office where I signed the papers and paid out the hefty fee to be able to move in immediately rather than wait. Over the next two days, the guys managed to help get all new furniture moved into the place, as Poppy had been marking things in magazines and saving shit to her Pinterest account that gave me an idea of what she'd want in the house. The whole process was tiring and quite frankly, pissing Poppy off every time I made a new excuse to run out the door. I'm sure she was having flashes of Walker doing just that and running to be with a club whore, especially since she was out of commission in the sexual department during her postpartum rest time.

She would realize what I'd been up to soon enough though. She'd had it with my shit, and asked if Leanne could come pick her and the baby up and get them out of the house for a little while. She thought Brantley was still staying with Kent, who had watched him and Bubba while we'd gone to Georgia, but he was helping out with the house, and excited to surprise our girls.

We had just finished setting up the last of the nursery when the sounds of a car pulling up in the driveway made its way in through the window that had been cracked for a couple days in order to help air out the fresh paint smell. "Dey Hewe!" Brant shouted.

"Okay, little man, calm down. We don't want them to know we're in here just yet. It's a surprise, remember?"

"Me Membas."

He put his little finger over his mouth and made a shushing sound that had Chief, Ghost, and Surfer chuckling. We all headed down the stairs and into the living room right about the time the door started to jiggle.

"They just gave you the keys?" Poppy was asking Leanne.

"Yeah, of course, when you're trying to sell a house you want as many people to go through them as possible. They just told me what time to pick them up and here we are."

"I thought you loved the house you're in."

"Um, well, I do," Leanne fumbled as she jiggle the lock, clearly unsuccessful with the key I'd given her. Ghost shook his head and walked over to unlock the door for her and then he stepped back.

"Oh, I got it," Leanne called out in triumph.

"That's good because this car seat is heavy. I never knew our little peanut was going to give me such a workout," Poppy sighed out. I almost chuckled, because it wasn't the first time she'd made mention of how much our little chunky girl weighed. She was already tipping the scales over eight pounds, but when you added in the weight of the car seat baby carrier piece, it became a bit more.

The door opened and everyone whisper-yelled, "Surprise!"

"Oh my God!" Poppy called out when she saw Brant and me standing there, but she didn't seem to be catching on.

"Welcome home, honey!"

"Welcome, what?"

"This is our new home," I told her and that's when she really looked around and started noticing things. Her eyes widened and I watched as tears started to pool there. Moving quickly to get to her side, I took hold of our little bundle, unstrapping her, and plucking her up from the seat and cradling her to my chest before taking Poppy's hand in mine. "Come on, I'll give you the tour.

She turned back to Brant. "Come on baby, let's take a tour," she offered while holding out her other hand.

"A seed it, Popwee. We puts all dis togeder."

"I see," she told him and then made a show of glancing around again. "You did a wonderful job, big guy!" She ruffled his hair as she said it and he reached around her legs, hugging tightly to her as he puffed his chest out with pride. "I'm so proud of you," she told him as she leaned in and hugged him back."

"Wuv you, Popwee!"

That was when she lost her battle with the tears, and they started streaming down her face. "Love you too, big guy!" Chief swooped in then and picked Brant up.

"How about we let your Uncle Smoke show Poppy around the house, okay? You can come have a beer with me in the kitchen." Brant wrinkled his nose.

"Gwoss," he muttered.

Chief laughed. "Okay, root beer for you and a beer for me," he amended which brought back Brant's grin.

"Wets go!"

Poppy turned to me once they were clear of the room, and not caring who was watching, she slipped up onto her tip toes and brought her lips straight to mine, planting the sweetest damn kiss on me. "Thank you," she whispered with her lips sweeping over mine as she did so.

"Anything for you, honey."

"I think you really mean that," she mumbled.

"Don't ever doubt it."

20. THE BELLS

Nerves had never been my thing. I always prided myself on not freaking out over too many things. I dove headfirst into fires to save lives for fuck's sake. There simply wasn't time to be nervous, but as I stared at the back doors to the clubhouse, my heart ticked away the beats as if it were trying to escape my chest. My world was turned upside down when I'd met Poppy, and now it was time to make her officially mine. Since she surprised us by delivering our daughter earlier than expected, just after her divorce was finalized, we had to wait a little while for our lives to settle into something resembling normal again before we could put this shindig together.

That's why I had a little trail of sweat trickling down my back. It sure as fuck wasn't the pyramid glass tube propane heaters the guys had placed around the deck to keep everyone warm. My palms were starting to sweat too. Hell, it wasn't even that Surfer was over there looking too cozy as Mr. Mom while holding my baby girl. Shit, that might have been part of it. I'm not too much of a manly jackass to admit that I didn't want anyone else soaking up my daughter's time. She was my baby girl, and so damn special. I was watching Surfer in his attempts to earn one of her rare and precious smiles when a hush fell over the crowd. My gaze quickly shifted to the doors that were now opened. Chief stood there in his Sunday best – which for him consisted of dark jeans, a button up shirt, and his kutte along with recently spit-shined boots. On his arm was my woman, looking radiant as ever in a simple blush pink sheath dress that hugged her curves that had been exaggerated by giving birth to our daughter so recently. I loved every inch of her beautiful self as she beamed one of her gorgeous smiles my way before looking down at the other man in her life. In her right hand, she held Brantley's, clasped tightly.

"I'm mawying Popwee, guys!" He shouted after grinning up at her. His announcement stopped both Chief and Poppy in their tracks as they laughed along with everyone else waiting to watch us become husband and wife. Little man was wearing an outfit that mirrored Chief's, including the little leather kutte my brother-in-law had made for him that announced he was a future biker in training.

"You better bring my woman over here to me, Little Man," I called out to him. He grinned big at me before he started trying to drag Poppy down the aisle at a faster pace than the wedding march dictated. More laughter ensued, and it filled me with a peace I hadn't known much of this year. It was good to see everyone able to have this day of laughter and celebration, considering the gloomy months prior where we had so much loss and took so many chances as we brought justice to our fallen family members.

I wish I could recount the vows we made to one another, but anything I said about them would be a lie. I couldn't tell you a single word I spoke other than, 'I do'. I was simply too mesmerized by Poppy, and the fact that she was about to be mine in every way. I remember her saying, 'I do,' and whispering, 'Love you always, baby'. Then I was kissing her and Brant was being Brant.

"Eww! Why deyz kissin' wike dat?"

"You'll be doing that with girls one day too," one of my brothers told him.

"Nuh-uh. Yukky!" We finally managed to break apart at that.

21. THE BOYS

I HELD DECKER CRADLED IN MY ARMS AS I REACHED INTO THE CRIB to pat Devon's diapered butt. Both were a little fussy tonight even though I'd changed them, fed the little piglets, and burped them both. The door squeaked causing me to cringe because the last thing any of us wanted was for Poppy to wake up. She'd barely been getting any sleep and it was starting to show in her crankiness. Not that I blamed her. Having twin infants, a preschooler, and then eight-year-old Brantley was nothing to shake a stick at. These kids were keeping us on our toes, and since I also had to work my shifts at the fire department, that meant most of it rested on Poppy alone while I was gone.

I turned expecting to see her and was instead greeted by my bleary-eyed eight-year-old. "Hey, little man, what's shakin'?"

"The babies, I guess," he told me as he rubbed his tired eyes. "When are they ever going to sleep at night?"

"I don't know, Brant. Wish they'd learn it soon."

"Me too. Sophie wasn't like this."

"No, Sophie still loves her sleep even when the boys are crying."

"She must be magic."

"Some girls are. She takes after her momma that way," I told him. Then I leaned in and kissed Decker's crinkled little forehead. "You boys happen to have the best momma in the world, and one day, when you grow up and become men, you'll know the only woman for you because she's going to live up to your momma's example.

"Can't I just marry Poppy, since she's so pretty and nice?"

I chuckled at that. "She's already mine, kiddo."

"Why do you get the good woman?"

"Because I'm smart, and I snatched her up the minute I found her."

"That's what I'm gonna do too. So, I guess it can't be Kaylee," he told me with a bit of a sad hesitation in his voice. "I didn't snatch her up. I just pulled her hair a little bit, and she ran away from me." He started tugging at his bottom lip, a sure sign of agitation with Brant.

I laughed again, gently so I didn't wake Devon who had finally fallen off to sleep. "Little man, one day you might just figure out that pulling a girl's hair and snatching her up to be yours are pretty much the same thing. If you want her, you just make sure she knows you're the only guy who gets to pull her hair."

I heard a bit of feminine chuckling from the other room and knew that my own woman had awoken and listened in through the baby monitor. I'd show her all about the hair pulling later when she had a little more sleep, and we conned

Chief into babysitting our brood again. Yeah, we had to count a babysitter most of the time to get any in this house full of heathens. Damn Brantley had some kind of special radar. Every time I got my woman naked, he came barging in like the little tike version of a cockblock. Hand to God, the little shit could pick locks. He'd figured out how to pop something into the hole on the door to get it to open up, despite the lock being engaged for a reason.

Still, as it turned out, my advice to our boys wasn't always going to be taken the right way. The next day Poppy got called into the Principal's office and refused to leave until I got there to sit in on whatever the hell was going on with Brantley too.

"Mr. Lewis," Principal Morris intoned as I moved into the room where Poppy was hiding her face as her shoulders shook. What the hell was so bad that my son had her in tears?" I turned to look at Brant who rolled his eyes at Poppy's display and shrugged his shoulders at me. Then I glanced back in time to see Principal Morris cover up a grin he'd been trying hard not to show.

"Brant, go wait out in the chair by the office door."

"But," he started to argue.

"Go, now! I had to run down here from the station. You know what that means?"

"Yes, sir," he offered up dejectedly knowing he'd be in deep shit later for me having to leave the station in the middle of a shift. I had a radio with me, and would leave this meeting in a hot second if a call came through for us, but that didn't matter. It would still set my team back to not have me on board with them as they rolled out.

Once our boy was out of the room, Poppy's groan caught my attention and I watched as she wiped a track of tears from her cheek. Then she looked guiltily toward the principal. "I'm so sorry, it's just," she could not contain her chuckling. "His dad's bad advice led to this, and I couldn't help it."

"Understandable, Mrs. Lewis," the principal consoled her and then turned his attention to me.

"What the hell is going on here?" I finally had to ask.

"Brant is being suspended for the day for assault on another student," the principal informed me.

"What the fuck?" I turned to see Poppy, still trying to contain her laughter. "Our boy assaulted someone, got himself suspended, and you're laughing about it." She couldn't even respond. I turned back to Principal Morris. "Who the hell did he assault?"

"Well," he glanced down at some paperwork in his hands. "A young miss Kaylee Swinson was on the playground minding her own business," he started and it was my turn to groan as I went and parked my ass in the chair Brant had vacated when I sent him out. "I see you already might know where this is going?"

"Shit!" I huffed out. "What did he do?"

"Brantley marched right over to her, yanked her ponytail and kept hold of it until the girl was forced to look at him, and then said," he shuffled a paper out of the way. "Ah, here it is," he glanced up at me with a grin. "I'm quoting here, 'I'm the only guy who gets to pull your hair, Kaylee. You're my girl. I'm snatching you up.'"

I noticed Principal Morris appeared to have more to say on the matter and I sighed deeply. "What else?"

"Mrs. Shelton tried to intervene and get him to let go of Kaylee's hair, but he refused." He eyeballed me then before continuing. "I'm quoting here again, 'My dad said that's how you gotta claim your woman this way!' was his defense when Mrs. Shelton tried to get him to stop, and asked why he wouldn't let go."

"Jesus!" I huffed out. First of all, it was the first time Brant had acknowledged me as his dad. I'd seen him think about it a time or two as the twins had arrived and Sophie had grown old enough to call out for her daddy whenever she wasn't getting her way with someone else in the house. My heart physically squeezed tighter in my chest as that sunk in. Then I had to laugh, because I had basically told him that. I just didn't think he'd run with it so literally.

"Mrs. Lewis thought it best if you heard it from me, rather than dealing with the situation on her own. She said that you had given your boys some creative advice just last night."

"Yeah, Mr. Morris, I did," I admitted while shaking my head in disbelief over the situation. "Just be glad the twins are still too young to take the shit I say to heart. You might have had three cavemen out there dragging their women away." Both Morris and Poppy laughed at that.

"What are we going to do with him?" Poppy asked through her laughter.

"I'm thinking we need to not let me give middle of the night life advice to the kids."

"That's probably for the best," Principal Morris stated while getting his own chuckles under control. "While I can see this was all a harmless misunderstanding, little Miss

Kaylee had a few strands pulled from her hair and was humiliated on the playground, so I'm afraid I'll have to insist the punishment still be served."

"I understand. I'll talk to Brant about it when we get home," I told him as I stood.

"Maybe, you should let your wife take over from here," the man told me deadpan, and Poppy started in on a whole new round of laughter.

"Yeah, you got me there."

22. ALWAYS MORE
THREE YEARS LATER

POPPY WAS STARING BLANKLY AT A WALL WHEN I WALKED UP TO HER after putting the twins down for their nap. "Maybe we should add on another room?" she asked the wall, not even realizing I had moved into the room with her.

"Why would we do that? The twins are okay sharing for now, and by the time they want their own space, Brant will probably be in his own place."

"Yeah, but where will that leave the new baby in seven months?"

"What?"

She turned to grin at me while holding out a familiar pink and white stick. It only took a quick glance down to see that there were two very predominant pink lines showing in the window. "We're having another baby!"

"We're having another baby?" I questioned while mocking her very words. I was stunned. We already had Sophie still running around trying to play little mommy to the twins who were getting big enough in their terrible three stages to resent it now. The boys were far too independent in their terrorizing ways to want their big sister to treat them as the dolls she seemed to think they were.

"Yeah, honey, maybe it'll be a girl to help even things out around here," she hummed happily. Another girl? Sophie was already showing signs that she'd be a stunner by high school. Not that she wasn't already, but she didn't exactly know how to match her outfits, and there were the big gaps in her teeth from where she was losing her baby teeth left and right. Still, those big green eyes of hers and the dark reddish-brown hair were going to bring boys to a standstill one day. What the hell would happen if I managed to survive her dating, only to have another girl coming up behind her?

"Are you panicking about another girl?"

"Have you seen our daughter?" I asked incredulously. "Her future dating life just played out in my mind and I can't imagine going through that twice."

Poppy laughed at me. "Stop being ridiculous. We have three boys, I'm far more afraid of how they'll turn out when they start dating. Besides, look at the influences they have. A club full of men, who are mostly all good looking and have their pick of women," she insisted.

"A club full of men who are all settling down with good women," I corrected.

"There will always be the younger prospects and members that they look up to. You know how club life is. Our boys will want to join the club too. Think about it. What happens when one day I show up with you to a party, only to see one of our boys, or more than one of them, doing things no mom should ever witness."

"Now you know why some of the old ladies stop coming around late nights," I chuckled.

She smacked my chest. "I want a girl!" The words came out of her mouth in a demand.

"Well, babe, I hate to break it to you, but you're already knocked up. I think you get what you get at this point." She didn't miss the smugness in my tone. I'd given her two boys at once last time. I was sure I shot another boy into her this time. "Then I'm getting a girl."

"Let's just hope you're only getting one this time, whatever it is," I mentioned after reminding myself that we'd turned one fertilized egg into two kids last time. Horror flashed across her face momentarily before she glanced down at her belly and her features smoothed out almost immediately. That was my woman. She had already fallen in love with whatever was growing in there. It didn't matter if it was a girl, boy, or another set of twins.

"We'll figure it out, no matter what." She glanced back up at me with a sheen of tears making her beautiful eyes sparkle as she spoke. "You ready to begin again?" she asked with the sweetest grin plastered to her gorgeous face.

"With you?" I asked and she nodded her head as she bit into her plump bottom lip. I reached out and pulled her close with one hand holding her lower back while the other sat gently on her belly between us. "Always, honey."

23. BACK TO THE END
11 YEARS LATER

Balls deep in some chick, with a firm grasp on her hair, while she was riding him was the scene I walked into when I went to go deliver the message from Poppy to Brantley. Hell, I was still trying to wrap my head around him patching into the club, and earning his road name, and now this. B.B. wasn't that original, but he liked it because every time someone used it, it was like calling out to both him and his dad. He'd been given Bender's kutte when he patched in, and while it had been stripped of all the patches Bender had earned or sewn on the damn thing himself, the only ones left were the club patch and rockers on the back along with one patch on the bottom right that simply said 'family' and then Bender's name was still sewn in on the front left portion that would hang over the heart when worn. Brantley said part of it had to stay so his dad could always be close to his heart. B.B. was born that night. The B from Bender's road name took first position and the B for Brantley took the second. It was a tribute befitting of both the men, and one I knew Bender would be damn proud of.

He'd probably be proud of the scene before me too, and no doubt, equally as traumatized as I was about to be after seeing our boy thrusting nut-deep, drilling away into whoever the girl was that he had riding him like a fucking bull in the rodeo. I shook my head and cleared my throat to announce my presence. In seconds, he had the bitch flipped over so she was hidden beneath him as he snatched the blanket over them both to cover his ass and any of her bits that were hanging out.

"The fuck, dad?" he shouted while throwing a glare over his shoulder in my general direction.

"Sorry, should probably lock that door if you don't want people busting in here though. I came to tell you that Mom needs you home tonight. She has news she wants to share with everyone."

B.B. groaned and I chuckled knowing what happened when you were balls deep in a bitch and someone started talking about your mom. The action he was getting was about to come to an abrupt and rather limp halt. It didn't matter that Poppy was only an aunt to him by marriage. She had taken in him in as a little boy and he had become ours just as much as he had been my sister and Bender's.

The feminine giggling when the inevitable happened let me know that's exactly what went down. It also announced exactly who my son had in his room.

"Message received; can you go now?" he growled.

"Sorry," I repeated the apology again even though I didn't mean it. Served the bastard right for all the times he cockblocked me getting with Poppy while we were raising him.

"Oh, and Kaylee, you should come too. Poppy would love to see you."

"It ain't like that," B.B. hissed as I heard Kaylee gasp, clearly upset with his response. Shit. I backed up, ready to get out of throwing distance, because Kaylee was a sweet girl, but one that came with a hell of a temper too. Hell, B.B. was responsible for some of her temper over the years the way those two went back and forth so much. Still, I knew better than to stick around for the show that would follow my boy basically announcing they weren't back together while still cocked up between her legs.

Those two had broken up when she left for college – his stupid ass idea – the year before. They had dated all the way through high school before that. We were all certain B.B. had claimed his woman the moment he met her all those years ago in grade school and pulled her hair. Poppy had been devastated when they broke up because she loved Kaylee like one of our own. Since I'd already ruined enough shit for B.B., I hit the lock on the door and closed it on my way out so that I could carry my ass home to my woman and our other four kids.

As we all sat down to dinner later that evening, Devon piped up immediately. "Are you guys getting a divorce?"

"What?" Poppy shrieked.

"Fuck no!" I yelled at him.

"Oh! Then what's so important? I had a date for tonight." I was about to reach over and pop the little shit in the back of the head, but his twin beat me to it. I tipped my chin at Decker in response.

"Well," Poppy blushed as her eyes traveled around the table making contact with B.B., the twins, Sophie, and our baby girl Haley before she locked them to mine. "You're all going to have another brother or sister in a few months."

Everyone was stunned silent for a few moments, me included, especially since we thought Poppy had been going through menopause or something with the way her periods were messed up, the exhaustion, and hot flashes. Then it dawned on me. Those were not menopause symptoms after all. She'd just been pregnant.

"Way to go, dad! Guess your geriatric sperm are still firing!" B.B. hooted out while offering up a congratulatory slap on the back. His evil grin said it all. He was about to try to get me back for his earlier embarrassment.

"What's a sperm?" My 11-year-old angel, Haley asked causing B.B. to double over in laughter. Her grin gave her away too. She already knew what it was and was just trying to make everyone uncomfortable. The little devil. I always thought she'd be the baby of the bunch forever.

"Shit," I huffed out as I turned my own special grin on the love of my life. It looked like we were going to be starting all over again at 45 and 49. How the hell had we managed that? "You ready to begin again?" I asked her.

"With you?" she questioned, to which I only smiled and

nodded my head at the silly woman. "Always," came her whispered reply.

THANKS FOR READING Smoke and the Flame, book #2 in the Aces High MC - Cedar Falls Series

Please read/review the book, as this is how other readers find the books you love.

Don't forget to check out the other books in the Aces High MC - Cedar Falls Series.

- Redemption Weather
- Proven

ALSO BY CHRISTINE MICHELLE

CHRISTINE MICHELLE

Kings of Anarchy MC: New Mexico

Property of Bigfoot

Aces High MC – Dakotas

Dancing with Danger · Whiskey Tango Foxtrot · The Restart and the Remedy

Aces High MC – Charleston

The Other Princess · A Love So Hard · The Princess and the Prospect · The Killing Ride · A Twist of Fate · Everlasting · A Year and a Day ·The Broken Beginning – Part One ·The Broken Beginning – Part Two

Aces High MC – Tallahassee

Crushed

Aces High MC – Sierra High

Walker · Trouble

Aces High MC – Cedar Falls

Redemption Weather · Proven · Smoke and the Flame · Redemption Duet Box Set

S.H.E. MC

Angel Girl · JoJo · Keys

Robeson Family Novels (standalones)

The Forgotten Wife · When the Last Petal Falls · A Different Husband

Standalone Novels

The Groupie Journal

Letters to Lily

His Bittersweet Regret

Bad at Love

TFO

The Fortunate Ones

T.I.E. Series

The Infinite Something · The Infinite Beat

Valhalla Rising

Revived

Dark Leopards MC (paranormal)

Ridden by Darkness · The B Team

Mirage Island Mates

Into the Grasslands · Beyond the Grasslands

Seasons Pack Series

Winter Wolves

The Ancients Series

Shadows of the Ancients · Falling into the White · Branches of the Willow · Bound by the Moon

Vukodlak Brew Series

Entwined · Enraged

The Awakening Series

Birthrights · Revelations · Incarnations

Death Viewers

Breathless

Upper YA Titles

The Voodoo Follies (PNR)

Catch a Falling Star (Dystopian Romance)

ANNE STORM

Savage Vipers MC

Wait For Me · Devastate Me · Surprise Me · Baby Me

Loved for the Holidays

Cupid Broke My Heart · Ghosted by Texas · Resolving Rumors

Cheating Hearts Series

The Homewrecker's Fate · The Regrettable Mistake

Standalone Marriage in Trouble

Nothing Special

ABOUT THE AUTHOR - CM

Christine Michelle runs on coffee and giggles as she writes her angst-fueled romance stories (motorcycle club, rockstar, paranormal, college, & other contemporary as well as women's fiction and marriage in trouble novels).
She is a mom to four humans (2 girls, 2 boys – all grown now).
When she's not writing books, she enjoys reading, drawing, hiking, or feeding her soul with live music at concerts.
Christine is a traveler and has lived all over the USA (and

other parts of the world). She currently lives in San Antonio, TX with her two fur babies.

Universal links to everything
(website, social media, book links, and more)
https://linktr.ee/christinemichelle

- facebook.com/M00nlitDreams
- instagram.com/christinemichelle_annestorm
- tiktok.com/@christine.michelle.books

www.ingramcontent.com/pod-product-compliance
Lightning Source LLC
Chambersburg PA
CBHW020633260626
47157CB00008B/2716